THE CAPTAIN AND HER MATE

ISBN 979-8-9955384-3-1

INDEPENDENTLY PUBLISHED

COPYRIGHT BY WALTER W. KING, 2026

LCCN 2026906302

The Captain and her Mate is a work of fiction. Names, characters, places, and incidents are either the product of the author's imagination or are used fictitiously. Any resemblance to actual persons, living or dead, businesses, companies, or locales is entirely coincidental.

To the women and men of our armed forces.

Thank you.

"Lt. Matthew Chapman reporting on board, Captain."

Theresa looked up from the conference table and into the impossibly blue eyes of the man she had made love to last night.

Author's note.

In the naval service, the commander of a ship, regardless of their actual rank, is referred to as "Captain" by tradition.

CHAPTER 1

"Uh, excuse me?"

Theresa woke up from her nap to find a Greek God standing over her. He was tall with black hair, a muscular body, and a toned butt, about 28. He was also, at this moment, embarrassed.

Whatever he wants, I hope I have it.

Theresa Leslie had graduated near the top of her class at Annapolis. She was the Navy's youngest ship captain, no mean feat considering the competition for almost any command afloat by officers much more senior than her. Granted, commanding the smallest armed warship in the fleet, the Patrol Craft Derecho PC-15, was no great honor, but it was her first command. Theresa found out early that the strain of command was a dreadful bitch. Alluring but demanding of everything she had and more. When Theresa felt overwhelmed, she often exercised, ran, or swam to ease the stress. She had no social life to speak of, just thousands of decisions, problems, and paperwork.

At 30 years old, Theresa was no slouch in a bikini. Her tall, fit body, honed by long runs along the beach and sessions in the base weight room, put many a younger sailor to shame. With her long brown hair cascading past her shoulders, she could be the epitome of the California surfer girl when she wanted to. In uniform, she was all business.

"Yes?"

"I hate to ask, but can I borrow your phone? I forgot mine was in my pocket, and my daughter just tried to call me." He held up his dripping wet cell phone as proof.

Well, that's a new approach, Theresa thought. *Men aren't usually that inventive.*

She searched through her beach bag, found the phone, unlocked it, and handed it to him.

"Thank you. I'm Matt. Matt Chapman, by the way."

"Theresa Leslie." *Looks like this day is going in the right direction.*

Matt punched in a number, and in a moment, someone picked up. He sat down next to Theresa.

"Hey, big girl. Did you just call? What's up? What did Grandma say? Then you have to do what Grandma tells you. Crying won't get you anywhere, honey. Put Grandma on."

Matt looked at Theresa. "Sorry, I'm taking so long."

"Don't worry about it. How old is your little girl?"

"Five."

"Hey, Ma? It's Matt. I dunked my cell phone, so if you can't reach me, don't worry. I'll be home in a couple of hours. Thanks, Ma. Love you."

Matt hung up and handed the phone back to Theresa. "Thank you, Theresa. That was nice of you."

Theresa propped herself up on one elbow. "Tell me about your daughter."

At last, ordinary people worries.

"Her name is Sophie," Matt said, leaning on Theresa's towel. "She is a girly girl sometimes and a tomboy the rest of the time. She loves to play dress up, but wrestles with the boys in her nicest dress. She says she wants to be a princess when she grows up, at least for now. God help me when she discovers boys aren't just for wrestling with one day."

Theresa laughed, "Sounds like you have your hands full. She's a lot like my niece. What does your wife think?"

"Annie was half tomboy, too. She wore beautiful dresses and jewelry when necessary, but she also loved tennis, golf, rock climbing, and other outdoor sports. She died a couple of years ago."

Ouch. Theresa thought—*a widower and his daughter.*

"Sorry to hear that. How has Sophie taken it?"

"At first, not well. She was too young to understand."
Matt was getting uncomfortable. "Do you mind if we walk
a bit?"

"Sure, I'll just collect my beach bag." Theresa got up,
shook the sand off the towel, and put the beach bag on
her shoulder. Matt took it from her and put it on his
shoulder instead. They began walking along the
shoreline, their feet occasionally washed by the waves.
Seagulls followed them for a while, making loud demands
from above.

"Sorry I brought up a sensitive subject, Matt," Theresa
said.

"That's Ok. It's nice to talk to someone. A few months
after Annie died, I went to the Pacific for six months. My
mom and dad live here, so they took care of Sophie while
I was away. I hated leaving her. Still, she's bounced back
and is full of energy again."

"What about you?" Theresa asked.

Matt stooped to pick up a seashell, brushed it off, and
gave it to Theresa while he collected his thoughts.

"I was a mess for a while. When I got too depressed, I'd
drink and email Annie, sending it to her old email
address. It made me feel like she was still alive, just
ashore. After a while, I realized I had to let go, or it would
destroy me. I started hitting the gym instead of the bars
and worked out until I could barely crawl into my bunk at

night. After my mom and dad got a computer, I could talk to Sophie and learn about her day. That helped a lot."

Matt stopped and turned to Theresa, taking her hands in his.

"I'm sorry, I've just been rambling on. I hardly know anything about you."

"I don't mind, Matt. I've got a good ear and a shoulder to lean on if you want one."

"Tell me about yourself, Theresa. Have you ever been married?" Matt asked.

"No. I have always been too busy and serious-minded for most guys. I was at the top of my class in school and college, laser-focused on getting an appointment to Annapolis. I dated some, but nothing serious; I ran track and played basketball. I always had the same goal in mind- the Naval Academy. "

"I bet you broke some hearts along the way," Matt said, smiling as they walked back.

"Not really. I never let anything get that serious." Theresa replied.

"Parents?" Matt asked.

"They retired to Florida a few years ago. We lived in Maryland most of my life. Dad served a hitch in the Navy, then went to work for the railroad. Mom kept house and did charity work. My sister Jackie has a daughter Sophie's age."

Two hours later, Matt and Theresa were showering the sand off themselves near the bathhouse. They'd walked down the beach and back together leisurely. Somewhere along the way, Theresa took Matt's hand without even thinking about it.

"Hey, if you don't have to rush home, how about I buy you a drink? It's the least I can do for your trouble."

"I'd like that, thanks."

Theresa covered herself with a light wraparound dress. Matt pulled on a sweatshirt.

Too bad. I was enjoying the view.

Where's your mind going, Theresa? You've just met him. Look, but don't touch.

They walked into a small restaurant, ordered wine, and spent the next hour chatting.

Matt was on travel leave from his last ship, a West Coast cruiser. He was glad to be on the East Coast now because his mom could watch Sophie during the day.

"My next assignment is the cruiser Raleigh, but it's at sea right now. It should be here in about a week. I'll be their weapons officer."

"I'm trying to get an old patrol craft back into service. It's been a real drag. I'm not sure they even make parts for those things anymore," Theresa said, swirling her second drink with a swizzle stick.

"Sounds rough," Matt said.

"It is, but I'm getting to know my boat intimately. Every system and subsystem needs TLC. I have a good Chief and a bright executive officer who is an electronics geek. We'll make do."

Matt looked at his watch, frowning. "I'm sorry, Theresa, I have to go pick up Sophie. I'm glad I met you today. Can I call you tomorrow?"

Theresa thought for a moment and then wrote her number on a napkin. "I don't take many days off, Matt. The Derecho needs to be made ready as soon as possible."

They split the check at Theresa's insistence and then walked out. He escorted Theresa to her bright red ragtop sports car.

"Is a kiss goodbye permissible?"

"Permissible?" Theresa shrugged. "Desirable?" she smiled," Absolutely."

Theresa felt a thrill go through her as he took her in his arms.

It's so nice to be treated like a woman, not an authority figure.

When her lips met his, a flood of pent-up desires niggled at her consciousness, leaving her craving more. She leaned into him, taking his head in her hands and prolonging the kiss. He pulled her tight, pressing his body against hers, igniting a fire deep inside both of them. Long-dormant needs raged, threatening to become unchained. His tongue pressed against her lips, asking to come in. She opened, and their tongues slowly caressed.

A car horn sounded, making both of them jump. They remembered where they were and separated sheepishly, moving so the car could go by.

"Uh, good… goodbye, Matt." Theresa stammered, "Call me tomorrow."

Matt replied, "Absolutely. Goodbye, Therese." He turned and walked towards his car, then stopped. He looked at her again and asked, "Would you like to meet Sophie?"

It was her turn to smile. "I'd love to. Friday evening?"

"Sounds good. I'll meet you at the dock around 1800?"

She nodded, waved, and got into her car. When he had gone, Theresa fanned herself with some papers, trying to cool off.

Wow. That was…

Careful, Theresa, this is dangerous territory. He's junior to you, she thought. She shook her head to dismiss it. *Don't be silly; you're just meeting his daughter.*

I can't wait.

***

The dawn was breaking as Theresa stepped out of her front door. The cool morning air made the first mile of her run comfortable. The path through the woods, an old fire road, was dark this time of day but easy to navigate if you ran there as frequently as she did. The thump of each step as she crossed the small, heavy-timbered bridge and the sound of morning birds were a beautiful background to her steady gait. She ran on autopilot, dreaming of her walk with Matt on the beach, holding his hand, kissing goodbye, and feeling his body against hers. She could almost smell his musky scent again.

It's been a long time since...

Theresa knew the day would be busy—she had paperwork to complete, evaluations, requisitions, and a multitude of other details a ship captain has to attend to. She hated it, but it was a necessary evil. Nothing got done without a ream of paper to support it.

She was starting to breathe heavier as she started up the steep, rutted hill to the top, her turnaround point. Deer, foxes, and other morning creatures ignored her as she sped by. The morning run was her time, a way to prepare herself for the day's meetings ashore before brass hats, supply officers, and the innumerable other bureaucrats that make the navy run drained her energy. She was dead tired each night when her head hit her pillow. Often, a wave of details and what needed to be done the next day wouldn't let her sleep. The memory of spending Sunday with Matt and the anticipation of seeing him again on Friday made everything bearable. As she turned back onto her street, Theresa began sprinting to the finish line, her mailbox, powering through the last few yards as fast as she could.

Time for a shower, coffee, and some yogurt, then work.

*****

"Commander Leslie, what do you think?" the base commander asked. It was another of those interminable meetings, this time about the Derecho's engine's fuel consumption.

Shit! I was dreaming. Stay focused! What was the question?

The Derecho, PC-15, was the last Cyclone class patrol boat to be commissioned. After a short, hard service life, it was placed in the inactive fleet and scheduled for scrapping. In 2023, the whims of the Navy Department declared its service was needed once more and decided to recommission it, upgrading the original concept.

"The Derecho's engines are tired. They haven't been upgraded since I took her out of mothballs, so the fuel consumption will be higher. We took her out once to test them. They are still capable but need an overhaul in the near future."

I hope that's what he asked.

***

Theresa was elbow-deep in grease, helping a machinist mate with a pipe fitting that didn't seal properly. The navy frowned on their officers getting sweaty and wearing grease-covered uniforms, so, at least while she was aboard, she wore camouflage pants and a navy standard T-shirt. If brass came on board, the duty officer was supposed to give her a heads up, then delay them until she could make herself presentable. Pitching in, even with the dirty work, was one of those things a small ship's captain could do to endear themselves to the crew. Theresa was used to sailors staring at her, dirty and sweating beside them, and her obvious female attributes. On this ship, though, the officers and NCOs had unofficially adopted her and dared any of their underlings to say or do anything wrong. Her cell phone rang, but Theresa couldn't let go of the wrench to answer it, so it went to voicemail. When the fitting was finally sealed, she wiped her hands on her pants and retrieved her cell phone.

"Hey, Theresa, it's Matt. I'll be there in about fifteen minutes. See you then."

That was twenty minutes ago! Shit!

As she walked quickly to her cabin, Theresa phoned Matt.

"Matt! Hi, sorry I couldn't answer. Give me a few minutes, and I'll be right down."

One of the few advantages of being a ship captain was the cabin she shared with the executive officer. In a patrol craft this small, it wasn't much. She scrubbed as much grease off herself as she could using wet naps, combed her hair out, applied some deodorant, and got dressed.

I'll excuse myself when we get to his place and do a quick washup in the bathroom.

Theresa informed the XO she was leaving the ship, exchanged salutes with the officer at the gangplank, and walked over to Matt's car.

"Hi! Do you mind if I follow you? That way, you can stay home with Sophie when I leave."

"Sounds good," Matt replied.

They parked in front of Matt's apartment building and walked upstairs together. When he opened the door, a little girl streaked across the room, leaping into Matt's arms.

"Hi, Daddy!"

Sophie was five, all pigtails and crinolines. After kissing Matt, she looked at Theresa, eyeing her suspiciously. "Who's that?"

"I'm Miss Theresa. You must be Sophie. Daddy has told me so much about you!"

Behind them, an older lady, obviously Matt's mom, rose from the couch and came over.

"Hi, I'm Beverly," she said, taking her cap and placing it on the hallway table. "Come on in. Sophie and I were having a big girl talk with Zelda."

Theresa looked around for another child before remembering Matt telling her Zelda was invisible.

"I haven't met Zelda, Sophie; why don't you introduce us?" Theresa said.

Sophie climbed down from Matt's arms, took Theresa's hand, and formally introduced her friend Zelda.

"You smell funny," Sophie said as they walked towards the couch.

Matt blanched, waiting for Theresa to explode. Instead, Theresa showed Sophie her hands.

"See my fingernails? That's grease. I was working on my boat before I came here."

"You have a boat?" Sophie asked, her eyes big.

"Uh-huh, a big one. Maybe Daddy and I will show it to you sometime."

 Theresa babysat for her sister occasionally when she was in port. Children being brutally honest was nothing new for her. She and Sophie struck up a conversation with Zelda while Matt said goodbye to his mom.

"Thanks, Mom."

Beverly spoke quietly," Do you want me to take Sophie home with me so you and Theresa can have some quiet time together?" Matt could see the double meaning in her eyes.

"It's not like that, Mom. Theresa and I just met," he said defensively.

"Sure," Beverly replied. "You never bring girls home on a first date."

"Mom!"

Beverly laughed, pecked him on the cheek, and left.

Matt turned to see Theresa sitting on the floor as demurely as possible, having a make-believe tea party with Sophie and Zelda.

Sophie never warms up to people that fast, he thought.

***

"It's eight o'clock, Sophie—time for bed. Say goodnight to Miss Theresa," Matt said. Sophie started protesting that it was too early to go to bed. "I'm a big girl now!" she stated firmly.

"Well, do big girls still like bedtime stories?" Theresa asked.

Sophie's eyes lit up as she nodded vigorously.

"Listen to Daddy, and I'll tell you a story and tuck you in, OK?"

Sophie flew to the bathroom, got undressed, and was brushing her teeth with the door wide open.

"She is absolutely precious, Matt," Theresa said, smiling broadly at him.

"You have a way with kids, Therese."

"I love kids. I never had time for them myself, but maybe someday." Theresa said.

Sophie came out of the bathroom, grabbed Matt's hand, and walked toward her room. Theresa stood in the doorway as Matt tucked her in and kissed her good night. Sophie eyed Theresa quietly and then held out her favorite bedtime story book to her.

Sophie tried bravely, but the day's excitement faded quickly, and she was asleep before the story was done. Her last effort was to hug Theresa as she tucked her in.

"Night, night, Sophie," Theresa said softly as they shut off the light and closed her door.

Theresa looked at her watch. "I should be getting back to the boat, Matt. Thank you for a lovely evening."

"Not so fast, Ma'am. Dinner awaits." Matt said, his arm making a grand sweeping gesture, beckoning her to follow him to the dining room.

Theresa looked at him curiously as he walked through the curtains onto the patio. When he came back, he pulled the curtains aside for her. There was a small dinner table with two candles burning outside. On one side was a bottle of something in a champagne bucket.

Oh, wow! He really went all out for this! Maybe we can have a couple of hours of us time before I head back.

Matt pulled her chair out for her as she sat down. She looked out over the shoreline behind the apartment building. The waves shimmered in the moonlight, and a slight breeze kept the bugs at bay.

"This is lovely, Matt," Theresa said as he poured some wine into her glass.

"Being a single parent, I don't get much adult time. Your beauty dazzled me at the beach, true, but there are a lot of gorgeous women. The more we talked, the more I learned about you, the more I wanted to know. I enjoy just being with you. I want it to last all night." Matt said, suddenly realizing how that sounded. Before he could explain, Theresa held up her hand and said, "We are adults, Matt. I love being a boat driver, but it can be lonely at times. I enjoy just being a woman when I can."

After a light dinner, Matt and Theresa moved the table out of the way and moved closer together. The warmth of the night air and the wine gave Theresa a deep, relaxed feeling for the first time in as long as she could remember. All her tension drained away, replaced by anticipation. Matt put his arm around her, kissing her cheek. She cuddled closer, blew out the remaining candle, and set her wine glass on the floor. They kissed, softly at first but then deeper, harder, and more passionately. Theresa felt the fire starting to grow inside her.

I can't do this. I can't get involved with a junior officer. It's not right.

Theresa stood up, knowing she had to leave, but it was too late. She walked as far as the dining room before she stopped and turned back to Matt. He came to her then, taking her into his arms.

Theresa kissed him hungrily, her passion rising with each caress. She felt him unfasten her skirt, letting it drop to the floor. Theresa unbuttoned his shirt, running her hands across his muscular chest. As Matt unbuttoned her blouse, Theresa whispered in his ear, "Matt, Sophie..."

"Won't wake up until morning," he replied softly, kissing the tops of her breasts. She shuddered, holding his head to her, feeling his mouth gently exploring her chest.

Her whole body burned with desire. She gently kissed Matt's ear, "Sophie was right," she gasped, "I do smell funny. I need a shower."

"Tomorrow, Therese," Matt said, as the last of her clothes fell away.

***

In the depths of Matt's mind, he heard knocking on the apartment door. The second set, more insistent, made Matt groan and get out of bed. Theresa didn't stir.

He flung on his robe and started to the door, scratching his head.

Man, this place is a wreck.

Matt opened the door, trying to rub the sleep out of his eyes.

"Hey, what's up?"

"Lt. Matt Chapman?"

"That's me."

I'm Lt. Brady, the XO of PC 15, the Derecho. These are the papers assigning you to us. We have an emergency recall. Get dressed and get aboard immediately."

Matt instinctively looked to the bedroom. Brady looked too and saw a pair of female feet pointing down on the edge of the bed.

"Ok, XO. I'll dress and be at the docks in a few minutes." Matt tried to shut the door quickly, but Brady was already partially in the door.

"I'll wait."

Matt rushed to the bedroom and shut the door.

Lt. Brady took a minute to look around. On the balcony, there was a table with a red tablecloth and candles. In the living room, Navy khakis were scattered all over the floor and the couch. A pair of black lace panties and bra hung from the back of a chair.

It looks like I interrupted something.

When Brady looked further, he saw a female officer's cap sitting on the hallway table. The brim had a lot of gold braid on it.

There is only one female officer around here with that much egg salad on her cap. Commander Leslie. Aw, shit! This is going to be awkward.

"Lieutenant Chapman!" Brady yelled, "Can I see you for a minute?"

Matt poked his head out of the bedroom door.

"Sir?"

XO Brady said, "I'm going back to the boat now. If you know where any members of the Derecho crew are, let them know to return to the boat immediately." Looking at Theresa's cap. The motion wasn't lost on Matt.

"Yes, sir. I will. Thank you, sir."

Lt. Brady left quickly, wishing fervently that someone else had taken it upon themselves to notify Lt. Chapman.

***

"Theresa? Theresa, honey, you've got to wake up." Matt said as he kissed her naked back.

Her groggy voice replied," What? What's up, Matt? Let me sleep."

"Theresa, I'm sorry, there's an emergency recall for the Derecho. The XO was here to give me my orders. I'm assigned to your boat."

Theresa sat up slowly, trying to blink and clear her eyes. Matt couldn't help running his eyes over her taut body and the large breasts he had grown so fond of last night.

"How do you know?" she mumbled, last night's wine still fogging her mind.

"Lt. Brady stopped by to give me my orders and tell me to get to the ship immediately. I'm sorry, honey, I think he saw your cap."

Theresa sat there rubbing her face, trying to wake up. *Brady? Brady? Oh Shit. That Brady! Why didn't they call my cell phone and let me know?*

She got up and wandered the apartment, looking for her cell phone. She found it in her purse hanging on one of the dining room chairs. The message waiting light was blinking red.

Damn it!

Theresa put her code in, and after an annoyingly long wait, the messages began to play. "Commander Leslie, this is the officer of the day, Lt. Nolan. We have an operations immediate message in. You need to decode it, Ma'am. Please call back asap."

She looked at the time sent on the phone- two freaking hours ago!

There were several other messages on her phone, all saying essentially the same thing.

At least Nolan took the initiative to issue the recall. Theresa thought.

Theresa strode back into the living room, pulling her clothes back on as she found them. She was all business. Matt was on the phone with his Mom.

"Matt, I'm heading to the Derecho. Move your ass, or I'm leaving you behind!" He heard the front door slam as she left.

***

As her car sped out of the parking lot, Theresa dialed the officer of the day. "This is Commander Leslie. I'm on my way. Are there any updates yet?"

"No, Ma'am. The op's order is on your desk. The XO is getting propulsion online, and most of the crew is present."

Theresa said, "Fine. I'll be there in a moment. Tell the XO to prepare to get underway immediately." She hung up without waiting for his response.

What a screwup! I decide to relax a bit, and this happens. That will look good when the boys' club does an after-action review. "Female Captain off screwing a junior officer misses operational immediate order." Great.

Theresa pulled into her reserved parking space with a squeal of brakes and headed to the gangplank.

She went aboard quickly, saluted the colors and the OOD, then strode purposefully to the bridge.

"CAPTAIN ON THE BRIDGE," someone yelled. No one stood to attention, concentrating on their duties as required.

"REPORT!" Theresa yelled.

The XO walked over, "Ma'am, the engines are online, awaiting orders. Stores are aboard, but we are short on all types of ammunition. Fuel is adequate for four days if we don't go balls to the wall long."

Lt. Brady continued," The last of the crew are on board. Our new officer, Lt. Chapman, came on board right behind you."

"Good, XO. Stand by to take us out of port. I'll be in my cabin decoding that order."

"Yes, Ma'am."

Did I detect a bit of smugness in his tone? Like, he knows something that could ruin my career and is letting me know it?

She looked at him as if to say, *"You have anything to say, say it!"* When he didn't reply, she left the bridge to look at the "operation immediate" order in her cabin.

I'm just overreacting.

***

It only took her a few minutes to decode the order. She sighed and put her head on her desk.

Damn! Two hours late! Theresa reached for the phone.

"XO, advise all officers and NCOs to meet me in my cabin when we clear harbor. Advise the Harbor Master that we are leaving immediately under emergency orders and request that all traffic in the shipping lanes be cleared. Hoist the appropriate flags. Take us out." As she hung up the phone, she felt the ship's powerful engines wind up, moving them away from the dock. Derecho's speed was restricted temporarily by harbor peacetime regulations.

***

"Lt. Matthew Chapman reporting on board, Captain."

Theresa looked up from the conference table and into the impossibly blue eyes of the man she had made love to last night. She paused, pretending to look at his orders before saying, "Take a seat, Lieutenant. Happy to have you aboard."

"Is everyone here?" she asked.

"Yes, Ma'am," the XO replied.

"OK. Listen up. At 0200 hours this morning, armed individuals seized the LP gas carrier Frances Mahan after it departed the Marcus Hook LPG terminal in Pennsylvania. The crew was surprised and offered no resistance. Someone was shot and dumped over the side, anyway. We are the closest Navy ship of any size and armament capable of catching the Mahan. The XO will give us details of our supply situation, fuel, and armament status in a minute.

"As soon as we cleared the harbor, we went to twenty knots. We may go faster depending on the situation as it develops. Our mission is to overhaul the Mahan and observe until we receive further orders. A Coast Guard cutter is enroute, but even with their head start, we should reach the ship first.

"A Coast Guard aircraft is currently tracking the Mahan. They received incoming fire and sustained minor damage during their initial low pass. According to the aircraft, the ship is heading into international waters. That can change, of course. All attempts to communicate have been ignored. One brief message was received right after the takeover. Any armed response to the hijack, and they will scuttle the ship immediately. If they go through with that threat, we can pick up survivors. Any questions so far?"

"Ma'am, do we know why they took the ship and what its cargo is?" The engineer officer asked.

"LP gas in pressurized tanks of liquid, some ammonia. If they can touch that off, it will be a bigger hazard than the ship just sinking. As to why, I don't know yet."

"We aren't doing a hostage rescue boarding, right?" Deck Chief Simmons asked, a worried look on his face. His division would be the one to carry out any mission like that. All his deck apes were as green as their faces when the ship hit the ocean waves for the first time.

"I hope not, but let's be prepared for anything. Have the Master at Arms report all our small arms and ammo immediately. Make sure everything's clean and ready, if needed. I want a live fire, general quarters drill as soon as we finish here. Put all the gun and weapons crews through their paces. No missiles are to be launched. We are critically short of them. Main deck gun ammo should be OK. Repeat the drill without firing anything for the next two hours or until we are in the vicinity of the Mahan. Let me know if there are any issues."

Brady nodded affirmatively. Theresa continued. "When you are satisfied, rest the crew as much as possible. Food and coffee issue at stations, if necessary, bunk time if they can. It might be a long mission, and I want everyone to be sharp. As information comes in, I'll pass it along. When you get back to your sections, fill them in. That will keep the rumor mill from cranking up. Any further questions?"

"What about any injuries on board the Mahan, Ma'am?" pharmacist mate Carter asked nervously. He was the sole person in the boat's medical department. The "Department" was little more than a large locker with supplies for minor emergencies.

"No definitive word. The one they threw overboard drowned, so information is scarce. Be ready for the worst. XO, your report now."

Lt. Brady detailed the ship's situation, including ammo, food, fuel stores, fresh water supplies, and many other essentials a modern warship needs to run efficiently. While he talked, Theresa glanced at Matt to gauge his reaction. He sat there listening attentively, ignoring her unless she spoke.

A green crew, a ship barely out of mothballs with minimal supplies and only one short shakedown cruise under its belt, heading to face an unknown threat on the high seas. Just freaking great.

***

Aboard the MV Mahan

"Why did you pick the slowest tub in the port? This thing barely does eleven knots!" Ali yelled. "Ali," also known by his birth name Thadeus Lomax, was the leader of a small group of 'Martyrs' from Philadelphia, Pennsylvania. He was 30 years old and a native of Brooklyn, New York, with several arrests for a string of petty crimes and twice for violent offenses. He had been recruited to Muslim radicalism while in prison. A minor criminal all his life, "Jihad" gave him a chance to be important, to strike the "Big Satan" at home, and he was excited. When his group took over the Frances Mahan, he immediately shot a crewman and had him thrown over the side to show authorities they were serious.

Ali turned toward the Mahan's Captain, who was cowering on the other side of the bridge," Get this thing moving, or I'll start throwing bodies overboard!"

"It doesn't matter, Ali." A calming voice responded, "Eleven knots, twelve knots, it's insignificant." Mohammad Rahman, an Iranian Intelligence officer, continued," The US Navy or Coast Guard will eventually catch up to us. Just be ready."

***

"Captain," Lt. Nolan, the signals and RADAR officer, said," I've received notification that a conference has been organized for 1500 hours. Admiral Kincaid, the Coasties, and you."

Theresa looked at her watch. "Very well, that's about ten minutes from now. XO, do you want to meet me in our cabin around then?" (On a craft as small as a Cyclone-class patrol boat, the captain and executive officer must share accommodations. It is also their workspace.)

"Very well, Ma'am," Brady answered.

"XO has the conn," Brady announced as Theresa left for their cabin.

It's a good thing the sea state is calm; we are making good time. She popped a coffee pod in her coffeemaker and then sat down to ponder what the shore navy had in mind.

We should catch up with the Mahan in about an hour.

***

The admiral's staff lieutenant set up the multi-screen conference, introducing the attendees." I'm Lt. Hardy of Admiral Kincaid's staff. On board the conference is the Admiral, Coast Guard area commander Captain Quaid, Coast Guard cutter Taney Captain Fox, and his XO, Lt. Marks. On board the PC Derecho are Lt. Commander Leslie and her XO, Lt. Brady."

"Thank you, Lt. Hardy," Admiral Kincaid said." First, the overall picture. In brief, a hitherto unknown terrorist group calling itself 'the Jihad' attempted to seize several ships at ports around the US. Fortunately, most of the attempts failed, but two ships, the Mahan on the east coast and the Rose of Texas out of Galveston, were seized. The Rose is a tanker, and the Mahan is a liquid LP gas carrier. We have every major surface ship available standing off every major port in case more seizures are attempted. Derecho and Taney are the nearest ships of any size near the Mahan's current position not already committed.

"Little is known about this group except that they are supported by Iranian intelligence. Most of the men captured were amateurs, local converts with a couple of hours of training. Each group is headed by an Iranian intelligence operative who communicates with the other groups. He has experience with explosives. That makes any rescue attempt dicey. If any rescue attempt is made, it has to be coordinated for both ships.

"These self-proclaimed jihadis were told a submarine would meet them somewhere at sea after they scuttle their ships. You can imagine what would happen to the crews when they left. There is no submarine waiting, of course, according to the one Iranian operative who didn't kill himself like the others did. The leaders will detonate their explosives somewhere in view of the US coastline so they can get maximum TV coverage. The media across the country are to be notified where to be and an approximate time. Once the ships reached some designated point on the map, all of them would be destroyed simultaneously, all up and down the US coastline. Fortunately, only two ships were actually seized, but we don't know their scuttling points.

"The bigger problem isn't just the ships. If the Rose goes down, there will likely be a massive oil spill and fire. If the Mahan blows up, especially in a harbor or near a major city, there could be a catastrophic number of casualties.

"Does anyone have any questions so far before I continue?" Admiral Kincaid asked. When no one said anything, he began again. "Each group was armed with various weapons purchased locally: rifles, shotguns, and pistols. Two RPGs (rocket-propelled grenades) were also seized, so use caution if you get close.

"Initial talks with those claiming to be the leadership of 'Jihad' haven't yielded much, not even a list of demands. Ravings sent to the media outlets are not saying much, either. They are stalling, but we don't know why yet. The

President has authorized SEAL teams on both coasts to act.

"Derecho, you will stay out of sight and radar range. You will be given coordinates to pick up a SEAL team and their equipment. Work with their commander to prepare an ops plan. Commander Leslie, you are in overall charge of the East Coast operation. Understand this. The Mahan cannot be allowed to explode near a populated area. If it alters course to head towards the coast, you'd better be prepared to sink it."

Theresa nodded grimly.

"Captain Quaid?" Admiral Kincaid deferred to him to detail the Coast Guard part of the plan.

"Thanks, Admiral. Taney, you're to keep in visual contact with the Mahan. Don't get too close. Advise Commander Leslie and me of any intelligence you can gather. You are under her operational orders. Coast Guard air assets will be overhead to support you in any way possible. Drones are being spun up to take over surveillance duties. The drones have more time on station to keep intel flowing. How you use them is up to you, Commander Leslie. Helicopters will be on standby to provide rescue if anyone goes into the water, but that might make the terrorists nervous if they get too close. Taney needs to have a boat ready just in case. I'd prefer that the Taney itself not close with the Mahan until operational necessity demands it."

"Aye, aye, Captain," Theresa said.

"Understood," Captain Fox said.

"One final point." Admiral Kincaid interjected," Both ships have to be taken down simultaneously. We will coordinate from here. Details, times, and coordinates to meet the SEALs will be sent to you when we are through. Don't make them swim longer than you have to," Kincaid said with a rare smile.

"I won't, Admiral," Theresa said with a smile of her own. *When an admiral smiles, you smile.*

***

Theresa sat at her desk, feet propped up, taking advantage of the downtime left before they arrived to pick up the SEALs. The XO was handling accommodations.

Who knows how long they will be our guests.

She was thinking about what she'd said to one of her old classmates in the officers' club only days ago.

"You're a lucky bitch, Theresa," Margot had said. "Very few women get a command like this. Most of us are stuck on dry land."

Margot was Theresa's roommate at the academy too long ago for either to mention. Theresa had gone to the Blue Water Navy, but Margot was stuck on an admiral's staff. She was young and vivacious and looked great in a dress. If she were lucky, maybe she would dance and schmooze bigwigs in Washington, DC, so that the Navy would get more funding. Otherwise, she was moving stacks of paper from one box to another for the rest of her career.

"I'd take a slot on a tugboat to get out of staff work."

"I'll see what I can do," Theresa said with a glint in her eye.

The look on Margot's face would have killed any other mortal.

"Still, the way things work, you will get that old tub up and running, and someone else will come along and take it from you."

Theresa nodded in agreement." I wouldn't be surprised, just disappointed."

"Better get that blue dress you wore at my wedding cleaned and polish your pearls. There's a staff office job in your future, too."

That was my biggest fear then, Theresa reflected. *Once I'm stuck in DC, I'll never see the ocean again—twenty years of being eye candy on some congressman's arm. Now, fate has given me a chance to do something useful. Take my boat into a potential combat situation in support of the SEALs. Maybe sinking an LP gas hauler with a ship-to-ship missile. I can't imagine how big that fireball would be. If they manage to blow it up themselves, that Coast Guard cutter will be doomed.*

At least for now, the blue dress can wait.

***

The special operations helicopter hovered ten feet off the waves. One by one, the SEALs dropped into the water, along with their gear. The ship's boat from the Derecho picked them up, taking them aboard the patrol craft. Lt. Brady met them as they came aboard, showing them where they could stow their gear.

The leader of the SEALs, an average-sized man with a shaven bald head and piercing brown eyes, an unmistakable air of authority, and wearing a black dive suit, strode towards Brady.

"Mark O'Brien."

"Terry Brady, I'm the XO."

They shook hands.

"I'll take my guys below and get them settled."

"Fine. When you're done, I'll take you to meet Captain Leslie."

In a few minutes, they were at Theresa's door.

"Captain Leslie, meet Lt. Mark O'Brien," Brady said. O'Brien saluted, sort of, and they were seated around the temporary table set up in the cabin.

Damn! Those pictures of her don't do her justice, O'Brien thought, keeping his face neutral.

The Captain and XO on a boat as small as this PC share a cabin. O'Brien looked around the cabin surreptitiously.

The only nod to privacy is a curtain between the bunks. It doesn't seem to be in use most of the time.

He looked at Brady in admiration. *You share a cabin with HER? I couldn't walk through a hatch sideways with the boner I'd have.*

"Welcome, lieutenant." Theresa said," I know SEALs have a standard operating procedure for this type of operation. What can you tell me, and how can we help?"

I could think of a few things, Commander.

***

Theresa was sitting in her chair on the bridge, staring out over the ocean, contemplating various scenarios, none of which had a good outcome.

The plan is sound, but things could go horribly wrong so fast.

You wanted a command, she reminded herself.

***

Matt was the officer of the day until midnight. He could see that Theresa was deep in thought and knew better than to disturb her.

This time last night, we were... It's best to stop thinking about that. The situation has changed a lot since then.

"Lt. Chapman, message for the captain," the sailor said, handing him a flimsy piece of paper.

"Thanks."

Well, I have to talk to her now. At least I have a good excuse.

Matt walked across the bridge and stood by Theresa, waiting to be acknowledged. When she realized he was there, he said, "Message, ma'am."

Theresa took the paper and read it. "Thanks, just log it."

As he started to walk away, she said quietly, "Matt, wait."

He turned back, standing so the other person on the bridge couldn't see her in the dim light.

"I'm sorry," she said wearily." Things are pretty challenging right now."

"I'm sure," he replied. "Anything I can do?" As much as he wanted to, he didn't dare touch her arm.

"Don't I wish," she replied with a wan smile. "I never expected both of us to be on the same boat. It makes things awkward."

Matt replied softly," I understand, Therese. I thought I had another few more days before shipping out on the

Raleigh. Don't worry. At sea, you are my commanding officer. I jump at your command. When we get home, though, I am going to ravish you severely."

Therese laughed out loud, attracting a startled look from the helmsman.

What could be that funny in a Navy telex?

"Thanks, I'll look forward to it," she replied conspiratorially.

Matt walked away, taking his station on the other side of the bridge.

I needed that. Theresa thought. I'll worry myself to death thinking dark thoughts like these.

***

"Coffee, Lieutenant?" the sailor asked, placing a pot on the table.

The planning session had gone on well into the night. Schematics of the Mahan's structure, as current as its last refit over a year ago, were poured over. Once the basic plan was settled on, the SEAL lieutenant borrowed the captain's cabin to brief his full team and refine their part of the operation. Little sleep was nothing new to him. As the operational tempo increased, he could expect to be running on fumes.

"Sure, thanks," O'Brien replied, filling his cup. O'Brien had a gift. Once a plan was in place, he could clear his mind and focus on other things. Excessive worry and self-doubt were not part of his makeup.

"Mind if I join you?" Lt. Brady asked before sitting down.

"Happy for the company," O'Brien said, looking around. "How do you like this old PC? It was designed to work with the SEALs, you know."

Brady nodded and replied, "There were fifteen, originally. Most were either sold to other nations or scrapped. Derecho sat in mothballs for a lot of years. We've taken her from mothballs to her first sea trial, but that's it. It's too soon to tell if it's going to be a good boat or not."

O'Brien's eyebrow raised. "It's operational, right?" he asked warily.

Brady shrugged, "Everything works, but we have only taken her to sea once—a run up and down the coast to check the engines and some other gear. We have the latest electronics too. We were loading up for weapons certification, but this mission short-circuited that."

"Right place at the wrong time?" O'Brien posited," A green crew, too, I bet."

"Twenty percent have been to sea before. The senior NCOs have been around. The captain and I are rated to stand deck watch. Twelve on and twelve off is a bitch. Lt.

Nolan has been shadowing as officer of the day until he's authorized to stand duty alone. Our newest officer, Lt. Chapman, has stood watch before on another ship, so as soon as the captain okays him, we'll have three deck watchers and one who may be released shortly after that. Don't let the newness of the crew throw you. We ran a lot of drills from the moment this mess started until we picked you up. The weapons crews are up to speed."

"That's something, I guess. Until someone fires a shot, though, you'll never know what they can do for sure."

Brady nodded in agreement.

I've never heard a shot in anger either. I can't let that get in the way. Too much at stake to worry about that right now.

"Have you ever done one of these, O'Brien?" Brady asked.

"A ship takedown? No. We've done it in training countless times, but in real life, we've boarded several ships underway that were smaller than this tanker. We secured them before they even knew what was happening. Not one shot fired. If everything goes to plan, you'll be amazed at how fast we move."

"Don't jinx yourself, O'Brien."

O'Brien nodded emphatically. He wasn't superstitious as a rule, but there's no point in tempting fate.

Mark sipped his coffee briefly, then leaned in to talk to Brady. "By the way, how long have you known Commander Leslie?"

"A little less than a year," Brady replied, pouring himself some coffee.

"How is she to work for? I've never worked with a female in charge before." The messman set a plate of pastries before them. Leftover from earlier this morning's meal.

Brady shook his head. "Don't worry on that score. She doesn't shake easily. All the BS we've had to cut through just to get this far would have made a lesser officer shell-shocked. Fighting for parts, wading through excuses why ships with less priority get drydocked first, and all the rest."

"No combat experience?"

Brady shook his head." None of us has seen combat."

"Few officers do unless they are on Special Ops duty like us. A big part of the Navy's job today is just showing the flag around the globe," O'Brien commented," being ready for combat, practicing for it, but never actually firing a shot in anger."

"True," Brady replied, pouring another cup of coffee.

O'Brien had to ask," How is it to share quarters with someone as beautiful as Commander Leslie? I mean, it has to be distracting."

Brady paused, considering his answer. He looked at O'Brien over his coffee cup coolly. It wasn't the first time someone had asked him that question, usually at an officer's club or party somewhere. He wasn't oblivious to Theresa's charms, but they had developed a good working relationship over the last year. He wouldn't endanger that by engaging in locker room talk about her. He chose his words carefully. "We aren't normally in the cabin at the same time, so there are no issues. If we are, we give each other space—as much privacy as you can have on a PC."

"Still, I mean, watching her change uniforms would be difficult. Sharing the ship's showers with the male crew has to cause problems. I bet they draw lots to see who washes the captain's undies in the laundry, too," O'Brien commented, smiling knowingly.

"I mean, if she were old, fat, and had warts, it would be one thing, but she's beautiful. That tight body and big tits are memorable, to say the least."

 Brady slowly set his cup down and leaned towards O'Brien. "Lt. Commander Leslie has busted her ass getting this ship ready for sea. The crew loves her because she isn't afraid to pitch in and get dirty. I'd advise you and your team to keep comments like that to yourselves."

"Ok, okay, don't get upset," O'Brien protested, raising his hands. "Can't get busted for thinking, though. Do you know if she is seeing someone at the moment? Might be fun to get to know her."

Brady looked over O'Brien's shoulder and motioned to a messman to take his cup. "Not now, lieutenant. Maybe later. The mission comes first." With that, Brady stood up and left.

What a tight ass. O'Brien thought, finishing his coffee.

***

Matt Chapman had been eating his lunch before taking over his bridge assignment for the evening. Sitting at the table behind O'Brien and Brady, he had heard everything they'd said. His anger grew, and his face darkened when O'Brien described Theresa so coarsely. He had clenched his fists and started to stand up when Brady caught his eye. His "Not now, lieutenant" had been a warning to both him and O'Brien. He followed Brady on deck to cool off.

Matt Chapman wasn't the only one to overhear the conversation. The sailor on mess duty told the cook, and soon, Lt. O'Brien's comments were all over the boat. Much like in the kid's game, his remarks grew and changed with each retelling. By the time the incidents began, things had morphed out of all reality.

At first, O'Brien didn't realize things had changed. The initially friendly crew stopped talking to him. Raw sailors on their first voyage didn't pepper him and his team with questions or declare they would try out for the SEALs as soon as they finished their time on the Derecho, like other ships' crews usually did. The Navy shower O'Brien took turned into a scalding blast of hot water when someone tampered with the outside valves. Later, a wrench dropped through an overhead hatch and almost hit him. His suspicions were confirmed later when he lay down on his rack (bed) and discovered it was soaking wet.

What the hell did I do? I haven't been on this tub twenty-four hours.

O'Brien wasn't the only one to feel the crew's wrath.

Team members noticed the crew had stopped talking and were staring at them balefully as they walked by. Friendly greetings were deliberately snubbed. It came to a head quickly when one of the SEALs overheard two crew members talking as he left the head.

"You just wait. If I have my way, they won't get an hour of sleep this whole patrol. Who in the hell do they think they are? Now the captain has to lock her door so these supermen don't molest her?"

The second crewman said," I have mess duty in the morning. Spread the word. Don't eat the eggs tomorrow. They'll all be sick as hell by tomorrow afternoon."

The SEAL team member, a tall, muscular man from Arkansas with a mop of unkept hair and a mustache, and usually one of the quietest, most well-liked guys anywhere he went, stepped around the corner to face the crewmen.

"Why wait until tomorrow? I'm here right now. Both of you at once, or would you like me to bust your heads individually?"

As he squared off against the two sailors, one of them produced a screwdriver from his back pocket while the other backed away.

Before the fight had a chance to begin, Chief McLaughlin stepped in between them.

"Knock this shit off. What's this all about?"

"Nothing, Chief. I don't like eggs anyway." The SEAL turned and went back to their team area. Within moments, every SEAL on the boat except Lt. O'Brien was primed for a brawl.

McLaughlin turned to his two young crewmen, backing them up against the bulkhead. "Ain't we got enough trouble without you two picking a fight?"

"After what they did to the captain, Chief?" one protested. "We can't let them get away with that!"

"What the hell are you talking about?" McLaughlin growled. They gave him the gist of the latest rumor. Both crewmen stressed they were only trying to protect the captain and the reputation of the Derecho.

"I haven't heard anything about that," McLaughlin replied, in a voice that only a Chief Petty Officer with twenty years of sea duty could muster. "I HAVE heard what's going to happen to you two if anything occurs tomorrow. Pass the word to all your buddies, too. You or anyone else start something with the SEALs, and I will not only let them beat the shit out of you, whatever they leave behind when they're done will be scrubbing this boat for the rest of the Goddamn mission, understand?"

"Sure, Chief, we'll pass the word," the crewmen said, hastening away before the Chief could think of something for them to do right then.

***

"Lieutenant, can I talk to you a minute?"

Matt turned around to see Chief McLaughlin standing there. McLaughlin was really uncomfortable. NCOs didn't like going to officers with problems. They usually took care of things themselves, but this one was getting out of control.

"What's up, Chief?" Matt asked, leaning against the bulkhead. He'd been hiding on deck, avoiding O'Brien, so he didn't punch him. Officers didn't punch other officers, at least in view of enlisted men.

I'm getting territorial, I guess. Therese is the first woman I've really cared about since Annie died.

"The talk about what happened to the captain is getting out of hand below decks. Some of the hotheads are planning revenge," CPO McLaughlin said.

What happened to the captain? I haven't heard anything about an incident.

"What are you talking about?" Matt inquired.

The CPO said, "Rumor has it that some of the SEALs tried to molest her in her cabin. The officers are covering it up."

Matt was surprised. "Chief, that's not true. When was this supposed to have happened?"

"Last night, sir. They broke into her cabin around 2100. The OD had to throw them out. Like I say, some of the guys are plotting revenge."

Where do these things start? I want to punch out O'Brien on general principle, but molesting the captain?

Matt crossed his arms, looking at McLaughlin in amazement. "Chief, that's pure bullshit. I was the officer of the day until 2400 hours. The captain sat in her chair on the bridge and dozed off around 2200. There's no cover-up. Nothing happened. Starsky was at the wheel; ask him."

"I'll make that clear to 'em, but some of the troublemakers are going to do something."

This boat isn't big enough to have that many troublemakers. It only takes one or two to incite others, I guess.

"Anyone who wants to hear it from the source, send them to me. The SEALs are essential to our mission."

"Yes, sir. Thank you," McLaughlin said, heading below deck.

The last thing Therese needs is a donnybrook between decks during a critical mission like this, Matt thought.

I'd better tell the XO and let him talk to O'Brien before it gets out of hand.

Matt subconsciously reached into his shirt pocket for the pack of cigarettes he used to keep there before remembering he hadn't smoked in almost a year. He sighed and went in search of Lt. Brady.

***

"That's the story, XO. The lower decks are exaggerating what O'Brien said. It's gone from a bad attitude to plots of revenge. If something happens before the Mahan is secured, the mission may be compromised," Matt said.

There were very few places on a PC where a conversation like the one they were having could remain private. The XO had been trying to catch some sleep, knowing he was in for a long night later. A situation like this demanded immediate attention, though.

A few more minutes and I'd have had a full hour of sleep, he thought regretfully.

First, I catch you screwing the captain; now, the crew wants to do bodily harm to the SEAL team leader for ignorant comments blown out of proportion. The life of an executive officer is never dull.

"Captain Leslie has enough to think about right now," Brady thought out loud." If I make any overt comment on this, she will surely find out. If I don't step on some heads, we may have a fight between the crew and the SEALs. I saw how you reacted to his comments, and that was based on reality. What do you think I should do, Matt?"

Matt paled. *I wouldn't blame the crew for wanting to settle scores if it were based on the truth, and so much didn't ride on the outcome of this mission. Brady has to know how I feel about Theresa, but he won't come out and say it.*

The truth dawned in Matt's mind. *He's making me sit that aside and think straight.*

"I think a word to the NCOs emphasizing that the mission comes first and that if anyone does anything to endanger that, they could be responsible for the death of the crew of the Mahan. I'd ask the captain to address the ship as sort of a pregame coach's speech, calling for everyone to work together to prevent this gas ship disaster without telling her about the trouble brewing below decks."

A tired smile crossed Lt. Brady's face. "Good. I'll have the NCOs in here after you leave, and I'll ask the captain to bolster her green crew's confidence by making that speech to them before going into battle. Hopefully, it won't come down to that, but realistically, bullets are going to fly any way you look at it. Thanks, Matt."

As Matt left the XO's cabin, he met O'Brien in the passageway, coming the other way. Despite what he had just said to Brady, Matt slammed his shoulder into O'Brien's chest as he walked by, knocking him into the bulkhead.

"What the hell is wrong with you, Chapman!" O'Brien said, squaring off for a confrontation.

They stood there staring at each other, waiting for the other to swing. Finally, Matt said," Stay away from the captain, asshole!"

O'Brien looked at him curiously." What the hell are you talking about?"

Matt replied hotly." I was there when you ran your mouth about Theresa. Thanks to you, the crew is about to go after your team."

"What did I say?" O'Brien thought for a moment.

All I said was...

"That's the reason for all this bullshit going on?" O'Brien said incredulously. "One of my guys almost had a brawl with two of your engine room crew who were plotting to sabotage our mission. I'm on my way to the XO now to stop this before it starts."

"Theresa is a lady, O'Brien. Not a Philippine prostitute, not a SEAL groupie, A LADY. Keep your hands to yourself and your mouth shut!"

"Lieutenant Chapman, I believe you have other places to be," Brady said as he opened his door to investigate the commotion.

"Yes, sir, XO." Matt glared at O'Brien for a moment, then left.

" O'Brien, can I see you a minute inside?"

What the hell is wrong with him? If he is on a first name basis with Leslie... no, a shipboard romance would be common knowledge. Maybe he has his own plans—too bad, Chapman.

When the door was shut, Brady turned to O'Brien and gestured to a chair. "Lieutenant, this is the small boat navy. If you say something without thinking, it's around the boat before you can understand what you've done."

Brady grabbed a chair, spun it around, and sat facing O'Brien.

"The question is, what do we do now? I'm sure we agree we don't want Commander Leslie to know what's been going on. Can you control your men?"

"I can talk to them, but they're pretty independent. They aren't likely to forgive and forget."

"I have to count on you to calm them down. Perhaps explain what started this mess in the first place. I'm going to lean on my crew a bit. See if I can get them focused on the mission first.

"We need each other, O'Brien. Your guys may be the best there is, but you can't do shit if you don't get there. On the other hand, I cringe to think of my raw green sailors trying to board and take a ship like in the pirate days."

O'Brien laughed at the thought." Something else we can agree on. Ok, I'll give it my best shot."

As O'Brien started to leave, he turned back to Brady and said, "As for Commander Leslie herself, I'll take that mission up again after we finish this one."

***

"That sounds a bit Hollywood, XO," Theresa said doubtfully, rocking back in her chair.

Brady agreed," It does, I'll admit, but with a green crew that hasn't worked together long enough to become a team, a fiery 'let's go get 'em type speech might help pull everyone together."

He's right. I should have thought about that. It's nice to have a good XO.

"Let me think about it for a moment."

What am I going to say? I've never been in combat, either.

Theresa nodded to the XO. Brady worked a few buttons, and the ship's PA system came alive.

Remember to be firm, positive, and loud. I have this under control. I have confidence in you, etcetera, etcetera. Theresa thought nervously, then put the mike to her mouth.

"Attention, this is the captain!" Theresa's voice boomed from speakers all over the boat.

"I want to update you on our mission. The Derecho is following the LP carrier, Frances Mahan. The SEALs are aboard to conduct a boarding operation and retake her. We will do everything we can to assist them.

"We were chosen for this patrol because the Mahan wasn't the only ship they tried to take. Another ship in the Gulf of Mexico was seized. Many of the Navy's surface combatants are guarding US ports in case more attempts to seize ships occur. The Derecho was specifically designed with the SEALs in mind. We are fast, well-armed, and well-suited for this job.

"I know we are a young crew and haven't had much time to shake down. For many of you, this is your first patrol. I believe we are a good crew and will respond to this challenge with our best efforts. Listen to your officers and NCOs. That's all."

***

MV Frances Mahan

Aboard the Mahan, the ship's captain seriously doubted his chances of completing this voyage. One of his mariners had been caught sabotaging part of the generator's electrical system before shutting off the engine's fuel supply. This would cause the ship to lose way and eventually come to a stop while repairs were made. Surprisingly, he had not been executed on the spot. The unlucky sailor was standing on the bridge next to him.

"I will feed you to the sharks!" Ali cried angrily. "Gather the crew so they can witness what will happen if they defy us again!"

"Sir," the captain said, trying to contain his fear, "This man is essential to running the ship. We already have a very small crew. Killing him will make it that much harder to operate the ship."

"Would you rather die, Captain!" Ali said, waving his rifle barrel under the captain's chin. The captain backed away, as far as he could, out the bridge door, stammering incoherently for mercy.

"Ali! Calm yourself," Rahman said as he strode onto the bridge. "Who is this saboteur?"

"Chief Engineer Sullivan, you wanker," the stocky, pugnacious Irishman said, glaring defiantly at Rahman.

Rahman returned the glare at Sullivan, then said to Ali," He's correct, Ali. We need a chief engineer to run the ship."

Rahman looked directly into Ali's eyes," But we don't need a captain."

The captain's eyes widened as the meaning of Rahman's words sank in. Ali shot him twice between his outstretched arms and watched as he rolled between the deck and the railing, falling into the sea.

"Engineer Sullivan," Rahman said, slapping him hard across the face. "If there are any further acts of sabotage or defiance, we will execute another crew member on the spot. You will stand there and watch him die. Understood?"

"Yeah, I understand," Sullivan said, looking down, his anger and bluster gone.

***

"The Coast Guard ship is moving closer!" Ali said. He picked up the RPG (rocket-propelled grenade), walked out on the bridge wing, and waited.

"Wait!" Rahman said, walking out to talk to Ali. "Let them pick up the captain. He's dead. Save the rocket in case we are boarded. We only have a few. It's our backup in case the explosives fail."

Rahman could see Ali wasn't convinced.

All you know is to kill, Rahman thought. *A useful tool when required. He must be handled carefully.*

"Ali," Rahman said gently, placing his hand on Ali's arm, "Why use our rockets to kill perhaps a handful of infidels when we may need them after we enter New York harbor? Thousands of infidels will die when this ship explodes. Put it down."

Ali relaxed, placing the RPG back in its case.

***

PC Derecho

"Captain! The drone operator advises that someone was tossed off the Mahan a moment ago. Radar shows the cutter is moving to pick them up," the radio operator said.

"Very well," Theresa replied, searching the sea with her binoculars. "Notify Admiral Kincaid. If whoever they are is still alive, maybe the Coasties can get some information from them."

***

"Taney, what did you find?" Theresa asked as she radioed the Coast Guard cutter.

"It's the Mahan's captain. He is in serious condition with bullet wounds to the chest. I have a helicopter inbound to take him ashore."

"Has he said anything?" Theresa asked, staring at the speaker as she waited for the reply.

"Negative. He is unconscious and on life support. With luck, the flight ashore won't kill him."

"Captain! The Mahan has altered course." The radar operator interrupted.

"Navigator! Plot his new course and project it out. Where is he going?" Theresa asked.

After a few minutes' work, the officer of the day walked up to her, handing her a slip of paper. The message sent chills down her spine.

Mahan is heading towards the port of New York. The estimated time of arrival is approximately 0800 tomorrow.

Holy shit. They're sailing a 53,000-ton bomb into New York harbor!

After taking a moment to compose herself, Theresa concluded her message to Taney.

"Good job, Taney. Keep me informed. Ask Captain of Taney to meet me aboard Derecho at 2100."

"Roger. 2100."

"Derecho out."

*****

"Analysis of the movements of Rose and Mahan suggests that Mahan was the big one, the Sunday punch. All the rest of the seizures may have been decoys. Each would have been bad enough by itself but combined with a 53,000-ton LP gas tanker exploding in New York, the damage and loss of life would be terrific. Bigger than that ammunition ship that blew up in Halifax harbor during World War One." Admiral Kincaid said. **

Damn. I read about that in the Academy! Theresa thought, appalled. *Everything in sight was flattened. Thousands killed.*

"That's not all." He continued," Even if the LP doesn't explode, its other cargo, ammonia, could cause chemical casualties on an epic scale if the wind is right."

"Oh my God!" someone said in the back of the room. The rest of the room was dead quiet.

"We've consulted with the President and everyone down the line to develop contingency plans. There are really only two possible outcomes to this situation. The SEALs assault succeeds, everyone gets a pat on the back, and a disaster is averted, or..." Kincaid paused," We sink the Mahan while it is still well out to sea."

Something awful is coming. Theresa thought.

"Commander Leslie, if the SEALs fail or you come within 20 nautical miles of New York or any other land mass, you are to sink the Mahan."

"Yes, sir," Theresa said, her voice choking with the order's immensity. Until now, firing a missile at the Mahan and killing everyone aboard had been an academic possibility. It was now a very real order.

"Twenty miles, Commander, whether the SEALs are on board the Mahan or not. If, for some reason, the Mahan breaches the twenty-mile mark, a flight of F-35s will finish the job, understood? That ship will not get anywhere near an inhabited shore. Destroyers based in New York are preparing to head your way as another failsafe, but they won't sail for another hour or two. You have the initial task of stopping the Mahan."

Theresa cleared her voice," Aye, aye, sir. The Derecho can handle it."

"The Rose will be assaulted sometime around 0600 GMT tomorrow. Your attack must happen at or immediately before that time. An environmental spill would be bad; thousands of dead or dying New Yorkers would be worse." The computer screen went blank.

Theresa sat deathly still, staring at the screen, rubbing her chin with one hand.

This isn't good. Only a couple of hours from now, the dead and dying will be stacked like cordwood somewhere. It's all up to me.

***

I knew it! She's folding like a paper doll! O'Brien thought. *Look at her just sitting there! Her first command, and she's going to choke.*

O'Brien and his team were crammed into the captain's cabin to hear the final briefing. The room wasn't big enough, and the temperature made everyone sweat profusely.

Theresa sighed loudly and turned in her swivel chair, looking at the assembled officers and SEALs.

"It appears your timeline has accelerated, O'Brien. Can you be on board the Mahan before 0600?"

"Yeah, Commander. I want to put a sniper team aboard the cutter since they will be so close. Our second sniper team will remain on the Derecho."

"Is that good for you, Captain Fox?" Theresa asked, looking at him and trying to act calmly. *I wish this coffee were ice water. My throat is dry enough as it is.*

"I'll take them back with me if they are ready," Fox replied.

O'Brien looked at one of his team members in the back of the room. He nodded and left the cabin with one other SEAL.

"They'll be ready when you are, Captain."

Fox nodded.

"Ok. This is what I have in mind. As far as the bad guys know, the Taney is the only ship in the area. They will expect any assault to come from that quarter or by helicopter.

" O'Brien, you take your boarders ahead or abeam of the Mahan, whatever you need to do, but on the opposite side of the Mahan from the Taney. While you take down the ship and your EOD (Explosive Ordinance Disposal) guys disarm any bombs you find, Derecho will stay out of sight. If things turn to shit, get on the radio, and either the Derecho or the Taney will assist. In any event, once you say the bombs are deactivated, Derecho will be off the port side to provide any assistance you need, and Taney will be off the starboard. That includes gunfire support. Between the PC and the cutter, we can make life miserable for anyone forward or aft of the gas cells. Any questions so far?"

"Why are you leaving the Taney so close if there is a possibility Mahan could explode?" Captain Fox looked around in annoyance. He knew who'd said that, one of his own officers.

"If Taney moves away or makes any move out of the norm, the terrorists will know something's up," Theresa said patiently. *I thought that would be obvious*. "That's the same reason Derecho isn't approaching until the last minute. Anything new might put them on their guard and cause casualties for the SEALs or crew of the Mahan."

"How do you know they are going to blow up that ship? An LP carrier has safeguards in place."

"We have to assume they have figured that out. Maybe it won't blow, but we can't take the chance."

The voice in the back fell silent, so Theresa continued.

This last part is going to suck, Theresa thought, dreading what she had to say.

"At 0600, the Mahan crosses the 22-mile mark. If it isn't secure by that time, Taney and Derecho will fire on the engine room in an attempt to disable the ship. Make sure your people are nowhere near. I'll give you a radio call first. I will start with the 50 cal. hoping to avoid fire or explosions, 25mm only as a last resort. That's the same if we have to provide gunnery support, OK, Captain?" Fox nodded his approval. "If, for some reason, that doesn't work or Mahan keeps drifting towards New York, Taney and Derecho will leave the immediate vicinity, and I will launch anti-ship missiles at the Mahan. We all know what that means. I suggest you unass the ship quick if we have to do that, O'Brien." A quiet nod was her answer." Saving the hostages would be great, but securing the bombs is the main focus. Any questions, comments, or changes? Anyone? Now is the time to speak up."

"I didn't sign up for this bullshit!" The same voice in the back said. Before Theresa could stand up, one of the SEALs grabbed the officer, dragging him from the room. A loud conversation followed in the hallway, punctuated by a not so soft banging on the bulkhead. Theresa scanned everyone's faces.

 It appears there are a lot of deaf people in this room, Theresa noted. She knew Captain Fox would be one of them.

The remaining SEALs were calm, their faces blank. This is the shit they trained for.

"Any OTHER questions?"

A few minor changes were adopted before everyone dispersed. Time had run out.

When Theresa shut her cabin door, she closed her eyes and exhaled audibly. When she opened them, O'Brien was standing there. She was initially surprised, jumping and instinctively moving away.

"I didn't think you were going to rise to the occasion," O'Brien said, opening the cabin door." When this is over, I'm going to buy you a drink."

Theresa recovered quickly." That's pretty presumptuous, Lieutenant."

"Just be there if we need you, Theresa," O'Brien said as he stepped into the hallway.

***

Speed and timing are everything, O'Brien thought as his inflatable boat skimmed over the waves toward the Mahan. *Too fast, and a RADAR operator or someone with a good pair of eyes might spot us. Too slow, and we lose precious time to take the ship before it breaks the twenty-two-mile mark.*

O'Brien had decided to come up the Mahan's wake instead of trying to drift down the entire length of the ship in the dark, as had been the original plan. He had to hope the terrorists were not professionals, looking at the well-lit Taney instead of the dark side of their ship.

The boarding ladders went up, noiselessly securing themselves to the ship's side. His team began climbing, spreading out. One terrorist stood on the deck smoking a cigarette and watching the Taney, a half mile away. He felt the knife as it sliced through his neck. Before he fully understood what was happening, he was dead. As the first SEAL lowered the body over the side, the second caught the rifle the terrorist had been carrying before it clanged off the metal deck. The pair moved forward noiselessly toward an open hatchway, motioning the explosives ordinance men to follow.

***

MV Mahan

They have to know where we are heading by now, Rahman speculated, patting the briefcase housing the radio-controlled detonator for the explosives he had attached to the pressurized tanks. *They may even have realized what we are going to do. The question is, what are they going to do about it? If I were in charge, I'd blow this ship out of the water now, hostages be damned. Americans aren't that cold-blooded, though. They will vacillate and negotiate until the last minute, then beg for more time. We will be in position to detonate this ship in a few hours, depending on the wind. Once we are close enough, they won't dare attack and risk killing innocent people. If they do anything to retake the ship, it will be before then. I'll blow holes in these pressurized tanks and let the vapors choke as many infidels as possible. Even if there is no fireball and no blast wave toppling buildings, the offshore winds will carry the toxic vapors inland, and hundreds will die, and many more will be injured. The fear that will be generated alone is worth dying for.*

***

PC Derecho

Theresa was on the darkened bridge listening to the infrequent radio reports that marked the progress of the SEALs through the ship. Lt. Brady marked off each compartment on a blueprint. One by one, bombs attached to the pressure hulls were located and removed. Matt was Officer of the Day again, standing nearby. The crew had gone to General Quarters an hour ago. No klaxons blaring or lights flashing. The green crew was already amped up enough as it is.

"Taney to Derecho! Gunfire on the deck of Mahan in the vicinity of midship."

Shit! Theresa thought, her hand squeezing the arm of her chair tightly.

I knew things were going too smoothly!

Every eye on the bridge was fixed on the horizon, expecting to see a huge bright fireball rise in the sky at any moment.

"XO, alter course to close with the Mahan. Full speed. When we arrive, take up our station and stand by for gunnery support missions." She picked up her helmet from the nearby console, placed it on her head, snapped the throat latch, and tightened the strap.

"Yes, Captain." Brady walked over to the helmsman, altering the ship's course and speed to meet the Mahan.

Matt stole a look at Theresa. While the Captain had the conn and the XO was working the ship, he had little to do. This was his first action, too, and he admitted to himself he was scared. He was seated at his weapons station, checking and rechecking the readouts.

Look at her. Calm and cool. Soft and kind to Sophie, tender and passionate with me, now a hardness I never knew existed.

"Captain, our weapons are all online at your command," Matt said. Theresa nodded, not even looking at him.

I pray to God that I don't have to launch any of those missiles tonight.

***

MV Mahan

Rahman heard the shot, then a flurry of shots as his men engaged the SEALs. He had chosen their posts well. Until the intruders killed them, they could not reach the bridge. Ali came onto the bridge, excited, firing his rifle at shadows Rahman could not see. He glanced at the nervous helmsman, a holdover from the Mahan's crew. He was still there, having altered the ship's course a few degrees, heading away from New York, according to the compass. "You are no longer needed," Rahman said, putting his pistol to the sailor's head and pulling the trigger. As the sailor fell, Rahman retrieved the briefcase housing the remote detonator and opened it. He punched in a code, turned a key, and pressed the button.

***

O'Brien heard the gunfire erupt on deck. He watched as the EOD tech was removing the last bomb from the side of the forwardmost pressure tank. The bomb suddenly emitted a high-pitched squeal, lights activated, and circuits closed. He squeezed his eyes shut, held his breath, and waited for the inevitable blast.

So, this is how it ends.

There was nothing else he could do.

When nothing happened, he looked at the bomb tech.

"I think I just shit myself," O'Brien said shakily, wiping his brow. The EOD man laughed. "Pretty close, huh? I deactivate the detonator before doing anything else. Scared the shit out of me, too, to be honest."

O'Brien patted him on the back before moving forward to assist in taking down the rest of the ship.

That's one of my nine lives gone.

"Sniper one and two, can you take out those guys by the bridge?"

"Sniper one negative. If he sticks his head out, I will."

"Sniper two, same."

Derecho, this is O'Brien," the radio squawked.

"Derecho, go ahead."

"I've got shooters on both sides of the bridge access ladders. Internal access is blocked; we are working on it."

"XO, how close are we to the twenty-two mile mark?" Theresa said.

"At this speed, twenty minutes," Brady replied.

"What about the hostages, O'Brien?"

"So far as I can tell, they've been dead for hours. They shot the engineer as we forced our way into the engine room."

"O'Brien, tell me when your guys are clear. We are going to light up the bridge."

The bridge crew on the Derecho turned and looked at Theresa.

Is she actually going to do that?

"Derecho to Taney, did you copy that?" Theresa radioed.

"Taney to Derecho, we'll start when you start."

"Affirmative, stand by."

"O'Brien to Derecho. We are pulled back past the first pressure container."

"Acknowledged."

Theresa turned to the XO, who was looking as pale as a ghost. "XO, advise the forward fifty mount to target the bridge area and open fire."

"Aye, aye, ma'am," Brady said. He picked up the sound phone and repeated Theresa's order. A few seconds later, they watched as streams of tracer rounds tore through the thin metal sheeting around the Mahan's bridge, rounds walking back and forth along the length of it. Taney joined the chorus with her own tracers dancing off the bridge structure.

Matt watched in awe as the steel came apart, the bridge walls shredding from the onslaught.

After a moment, Theresa said," Cease fire, weapons standby for further orders." The machine guns of the Derecho and the Taney fell silent.

***

Onboard, the Mahan, Rahman, and Ali were lying face down on the deck as the world around them filled with .50 caliber rounds. When the heavy thuds from the rounds finally stopped, they lay there trying to catch their breath.

"Ali, are you hurt?" Rahman yelled.

"No," Ali said shakily.

How did we live through that?

"Bring the RPGs over here."

When Ali arrived, dragging the case of rockets with him as he crawled, he said. "Two of them are functional. The other case is destroyed."

"Very well. Prepare one for you and one for me. Target the first gas cell. Fire as soon as you can; we will have visitors at any moment."

Theresa watched in disbelief as the smoke and fire trail left the Mahan's bridge. The rocket glanced off the side of the first pressure tank, leaving a scar in the insulation as it passed, speeding out over the sea.

Son of a bitch! "XO, fifty mounts commence fire. Target their bridge!" She yelled.

***

Ali screamed in rage, reaching for the second RPG. Rahman watched as he stood up and prepared to fire.

Suddenly, in front of Rahman's eyes, Ali's head exploded, showering a red mist as he sat heavily on the floor before falling over.

"Sniper one, target down," came the calm message over the Derecho's radio.

"Check fire, XO! The SEALs are advancing!" Theresa yelled, stopping Brady as he picked up the sound phone.
***

Rahman cleared his mind, reaching for the RPG Ali had dropped. When he stood, he targeted the Derecho instead of the pressure tank. He squeezed the trigger just as the first SEAL entered the bridge and stitched his body with submachinegun rounds.

***

O'Brien watched from the deck of the Mahan as the smoke trail from the rocket left the bridge.

Oh my God!

No one on the bridge of the Derecho had time to react. The rocket penetrated the thin skin of the Derecho (The PC was built for speed and was only lightly armored) on the hull below the bridge before exploding, sending shrapnel in all directions. Shards of metal and glass flew through the side of the bridge enclosure.

"Is everyone OK?" Brady yelled, ears ringing. Almost everyone was cut or injured in some way. As they resumed their stations, Brady noticed Captain Leslie slumped in her chair, not moving. Matt was by her side in seconds, "Theresa, are you alright? Therese?" Blood was running from her side closest to the impact point, but at least she was still breathing. He grabbed a small medical kit from the wall and started packing the lacerations with blood-absorbing gauze.

"Pharmacist mate, to the bridge immediately!" Brady yelled into the ship's intercom. He picked up the radio and said, "Taney! Do you have a helicopter on station? Send it! We have multiple wounded here. We are moving away from Mahan to a safe distance."

"Taney to Derecho, Roger, it's inbound as we speak. How many were injured?"

"Derecho is down, and several others are injured. I am assessing the ship's company now. O'Brien, how about you?"

"A few minor injuries. One of our guys caught the force of that last RPG launch as he entered the bridge. I have a corpsman I can send over."

"I'd appreciate it. Is Mahan secure?" Brady said over the radio.

"Mahan is secure, doing secondary sweeps. How is Derecho?" O'Brien said, concern evident in his voice.

"Breathing. The pharmacist mate is checking her right now." Brady replied.

"Ok."

"Hang in there, honey, help is on the way," Matt said softly, holding Theresa's hand tightly.

Brady turned to Lt. Nolan." Let Admiral Kincaid know Mahan is secured." Brady looked at the position displayed on the console by the captain's chair.

"Tell Kincaid to call off the F-35s, too."

During the prolonged engagement, the Mahan had sailed to within nineteen miles of New York.

CHAPTER 2

The last thing Theresa remembered was watching the rocket streaking right for her. When she woke, she was in a naval hospital, with tubes and IVs everywhere and monitors beeping.

The nurse picked up the phone and called the desk. "She's awake. Have the doctor stop by asap."

The nurse walked over to Theresa. "How are you feeling, commander?"

"Like shit," Theresa replied quietly. "How long have I been, wherever here is?"

" You're in the hospital. It's been about a week. The doctor is coming to check on you."

"What about my boat?" Theresa asked groggily.

The nurse shrugged. The date and the nurse's name, "Elise, " were written on the marker board in front of the bed. Below that was the name "Brady" and a phone number she couldn't focus on clearly. There was also an envelope, maybe a card.

Dr. Patel walked in, glancing at the monitors before addressing Theresa.

"Glad you are back with us. You had me worried for a while." He took a small flashlight from his pocket, looking into her eyes.

"What happened, Doc?" Theresa asked.

As Dr. Patel peeled back each bandage, checking drainage and looking for infection, he said," When you came in here, you had a collapsed lung, shrapnel in several places on your arm and leg, and a cut on your head. Fortunately, your helmet took the worst of it. You probably looked away at the last moment, and a piece of metal went under the back of it and cut a nice furrow in your scalp. It's above the hairline, so no one will ever know a scar is there unless you cut your hair too short. Concussion also."

He checked her urine bag for blood or pus and, finding none, turned to the nurse and said, "We can remove that as soon as she is strong enough."

"Dr. Patel continued, "You have been through two surgeries to repair your lung and remove some of the deeper shrapnel. You may have another one if the metal we left inside migrates. Other than that, I expect you'll be up and around soon and start physical therapy soon after that."

"Could you hand me that phone? I'd like to call my XO and..."

"No," Dr. Patel said firmly. "For the remainder of the evening, you will rest. Perhaps tomorrow. Go to sleep now."

With that, Dr. Patel walked out, already enroute to see another patient.

"Dr. Patel is a good surgeon. His bedside manner is a bit curt. Don't worry. I'll call Brady and let him know you are awake."

"Could you call someone else, too, please? He's my..." Theresa began.

What is he, exactly? We didn't have much time to find out. Boyfriend? Lover? Something else? All I know is I want to see him so very much.

"Friend," Theresa finished. She gave the nurse Matt's phone number, took the sleeping pill she was offered, and slipped into a deep, restful sleep.

***

The next morning, Theresa was reading the card from her marker board. It was from O'Brien, of all people.

Off on another assignment. I asked the nurse to give this to you when you woke up. I still want to buy you that drink sometime.

Mark

The front of the card featured a cute little dog lying in a hospital bed, with bandages on its head and a thermometer protruding from its mouth. Another dog, dressed in a nurse's outfit, was holding a bedpan. It said, "Let me know how it all comes out." She shook her head, laughing.

He certainly has guts.

Theresa's phone rang. The day nurse handed it to her and then left, closing her door.

"Commander Leslie? It's Brady. How are you feeling?"

"Like shit. What's the damage?"

"Everyone on the bridge and forward gun mounts sustained shrapnel injuries. Not major ones, fortunately. You were the worst. The Coasties stood by the Mahan until a relief crew arrived. You were flown to shore, and Derecho followed. The damage to the ship isn't as bad as it looks. We have to wait our turn for repairs, but she is afloat and seaworthy.

"Matt wouldn't leave your side. He'd have been in the chopper if there had been room."

"XO, why haven't you said anything about finding Matt and I together that day?" Theresa asked guardedly.

"Commander, I was carrying Matt's orders, assigning him to the Derecho. You had no way to know about his being assigned to our boat, so I figure you haven't done anything wrong."

"There's still the matter of his being junior to me."

Brady replied," I considered that. The way you pulled that boat together and pulled off a pretty tough assignment in such a short time, I figured I'd leave that between the two of you. You're a great boat captain, Commander. Besides, the crew would lynch me if they found out I stood in the way of your happiness."

Theresa chuckled at that." Why don't you stop by later, Terry?"

"Thank you, Commander. Maybe tomorrow. I'm overseeing the repair of the Derecho. Besides, the doctor said only two visitors at a time, and that slot is already filled. Goodbye for now."

Theresa was curious about that last remark until there was a knock on her door. It opened slowly, and Matt stuck his head in. Seeing no one else in the room, he said," Hi, gorgeous. Are you decent?"

Theresa's face lit up with a smile. "Hospital decent. Come on in; this gown is drafty enough."

"Too bad. Someone else is here to see you," Matt said. At that, Sophie pushed the door open and flew into the room, a bright red "Get Well" balloon streaming behind her.

"Miss Theresa!" she yelled in glee, climbing up to sit on her lap and hug her. Theresa winced in pain but returned the hug, kissing Sophie on the face. When she looked back at Matt, all he could do was say, "Sorry."

"Are you kidding? This is the best medicine ever!" Theresa smiled, kissing him as he leaned down.

Sophie looked at all the monitors, tubes, bandages, and other hospital things, forgetting that the balloon she had was for Theresa.

"All this stuff. You must have been hurt pretty bad," Matt said dryly.

"Yeah, I think my bikini body isn't going to be the same after this," Theresa said regretfully.

"Don't worry about that. Get well first; that's more important."

***

In the week that followed, Theresa had plenty of time to think. Matt and Sophie visited as often as they could. She enjoyed these times, listening to Sophie tell her everything that had happened since the last visit, including her classmates at school and what she and Zelda had done. Matt and Brady kept her apprised of the goings on onboard the Derecho. All this was wonderful and helped keep her mood up, but one thing kept her on edge.

What's next?

One day, Admiral Kincaid visited. Theresa struggled to stand up from her wheelchair as he entered her room.

"As you were, Commander. Relax, that's an order." He waved to his staff officers to stay outside and then sank into the one chair in the room. Admiral Kincaid was in his late fifties. Though he tried to maintain his weight and exercised when he could, age and years of desk work were starting to take their toll.

"How are you feeling now that the worst is past?"

"Better and better, sir. I'll be back at work soon," Theresa replied.

"Good. I can use a clear-thinking officer on my staff," Kincaid said.

This is what had caused Theresa the most worry. Her friend Margot had been right. Once she left the Blue Water Navy, she would be unlikely to return to sea again, certainly not as a ship driver.

"Sir, if I may. I hoped to stay aboard the Derecho and ensure she passed all of her trials. She's still waiting for a permanent fix to her hull."

Kincaid was direct," You are in no shape for a sea command right now. You still have a lot of healing to do. Lt. Brady is doing a fine job getting the minor repairs done. I'm thinking of giving him the Derecho and a promotion."

He could see the disappointment in Theresa's face. "Nothing is set in stone yet. A temporary assignment to my staff will do you a world of good. You can make all your doctor's appointments and have regular hours for a few months at least." He stood up to go. "When you are well enough, I'll have you talk to junior officers about the incident. Give them some insight into the demands of having your own command. Some Congressmen and Senators would like to meet you as well.

"This Friday, there will be a ceremony on board the Derecho. I'll have some awards and medals to pass around. If you are able, I'd like you to be there to accept the Unit Citation."

That brought a smile to Theresa's face." I'll be happy to, sir. The crew did a hell of a job."

As the Admiral turned to walk out the door, Theresa made a monumental effort to get to her feet. She was standing there shakily when he turned to say goodbye.

"At ease, Commander. I'll see you Friday."

That is one determined lady.

Theresa sat down in the wheelchair heavily. Sharp pains all over her body warned her not to do that again anytime soon.

This is how it begins—my transformation from the Blue Water Navy to the Blue Dress Navy. If I fight it, Brady may lose his promotion and his chance at a first command of his own. I can't do that to him.

***

That evening, Matt and Sophie arrived early. Matt had brought her a pair of white satin pajamas and some slippers. "Can't have you going outside with your ass hanging out," he said. Matt had convinced the doctors to let him take her to a nearby playground so long as she didn't exert herself. The nurses' assistants helped Theresa get dressed.

The playground was across the street from the hospital. It was brightly colored and had all the modern safety features of any playground. It was even handicap accessible, which Matt appreciated since he didn't have to drag the wheelchair up steps. They watched Sophie run around with other kids her age, screaming, falling, and having a good time. It was nice to be out in the cool, fresh air again.

Watching Matt push Sophie on the swing brought a warm feeling to her heart.

She promised herself,

Someday, someday soon, I'll be doing that.

"Thanks, Matt. I needed to get out of there for a while," Theresa said.

"You're welcome. My end goal is to have them let me take you home," Matt replied. "I want to take care of you."

"We can't do that, Matt. There would be talk, and eventually, I'd have to answer some rather awkward questions, "Theresa said.

"This is so damn aggravating!" Matt said in frustration, leaning back on the park bench and exhaling loudly.

Theresa nodded," No one said you and Sophie couldn't visit, maybe even... spend the night, occasionally."

Matt smiled at that. "Someone has to change your bandages, maybe kiss your boo-boos."

Theresa's voice sobered," It doesn't look like I'm going back to sea, Matt. Admiral Kincaid wants me on his staff. He's giving Brady the Derecho."

"Damn, Therese. I'm sorry. I know how much the Derecho means to you," Matt replied, caressing her shoulder.

"I was luckier than most. I got to command a boat in action. I couldn't put off a staff job forever. Still, I'd like to have stayed at sea longer."

Theresa locked the wheels of her wheelchair and began to stand up.

"Therese, don't! The doctors said to take it easy," Matt said, reaching for her.

Theresa managed to stand up and stood there swaying. Her face was sweating, and she was a little dizzy but determined.

"Friday, there is an awards ceremony on the Derecho. I'm going to walk to the podium to accept the unit citation. I'll take Sophie on a tour before we leave. I promised her. My crew is going to see their captain walking!"

Her wounds were healing nicely. The doctor who had sewn her up had done a good job of hiding most of the scars. Breathing hurt a little, but she wouldn't own up to it. Against the doctor's advice, she would get out of bed every day, twice a day, and walk, if only to the bathroom. It was painful and drained her limited energy. A sympathetic nurse found a set of crutches for her. By Thursday, she could walk up and down the hallway, taking frequent breaks along the way. She couldn't manage stairs.

Matt took her to her house and helped her get her dress white uniform together.

"Brady assigned me to be your assistant while you are in the hospital. The dock workers are taking over the boat, so I'm just in the way right now. I still stand deck watch, so I have to be back on board later."

"Terry is going to be a good boat driver. He thinks of everything." Theresa said.

"Is Sophie coming to the ceremony? Did you get her out of school for the day? I promised her I'd show her my boat."

"The principal said it was ok. You can show her the Derecho, provided you take it easy. I push you everywhere so you can save your strength."

"Agreed," Theresa said. "While we are here, let's sit a while." Matt pushed her to the living room and helped her to the couch. He sat down beside her. Theresa pulled his face to her, giving him a long, gentle kiss.

"I've wanted to do that for so long," she said. Matt put his arms around her, squeezing gently. "Don't start something you can't finish yet."

"Who says I can't!" Therese said saucily.

"I do. I have you all to myself for the next few hours, and I'm going to make the most of it. I may even paint your nails if you ask me nicely."

"Oh, you would, would you? I dare you," Theresa laughed.

"Wait here." Matt bounded up the steps, returning with assorted colors and brushes. He selected a nail file and started smoothing and shaping her fingernails. He expertly applied the paint next, allowing it plenty of time to dry while he started on Theresa's toes.

"I don't believe it. Matt, where did you learn to do this?" Theresa said. "They look great."

"I'm not done yet," he said, carefully painting her big toe." I used to do this for Annie when we first got married."

"I'm sorry, Matt. I didn't want to stir up any bad memories."

Matt replied, blowing on the paint. "You didn't. Annie was my first love, and it hurt me badly when she died. It took a long time to get my mind right afterward. Sophie is my saving grace. As long as I have her, I still have a little piece of Annie.

"After a while, I knew I had to move on. I still keep in touch with Annie's parents. Sophie loves her grandma and grandpop Roe."

"I understand, Matt. I wouldn't have it any other way."

Matt smiled and kept working, gesturing with the brush, "This started as a joke, just like your dare. Before long, I was doing it all the time, especially when Annie was pregnant with Sophie. I did it for her in the hospital, too, just before she died. The smile on her face lifted my spirits. Sophie was too young to remember that at the time. When she gets married, I'm painting her nails for her wedding—keeping the family tradition going."

And now me. Theresa thought, yawning—a *weapons officer who does nails. No one would believe it.*

Matt helped her lie down on the couch, covering her with a quilt. "Done. Now take a nap, but don't mess up your nails; they're almost dry."

Theresa smiled. *I could get used to this.*

Theresa woke up slowly. It was dark out and time for Matt to take her back to the hospital. "Matt, wait over there by the door," Theresa said. She stood up and walked to him, lowering herself into the wheelchair.

"Nice. Let's see you do that tomorrow with shoes on." Matt said appreciatively.

Matt had to leave Theresa's hospital room as two nurses' aides helped her prepare for bed.

"Who does your nails, commander?" one of the girls said. Theresa laughed. "You wouldn't believe me."

"That is a professional job. What does the writing mean?"

"Writing?" Theresa asked. There was none on her fingernails.

"No, your big toes," she said. "It says PC 15."

Matt laughed as Theresa squealed in delight. "That's my boat!"

***

Friday morning, 0900. Matt helped Theresa out of the car and into the wheelchair. Both were dressed in their white dress uniforms. Sophie was wearing a white dress, too, but she insisted on her church outfit, complete with a matching hat and stockings. The crew gathered around, saluting and enthusiastically welcoming Theresa as Matt pushed her to a place near the podium.

Lt. Brady yelled," Fall in!" The crew moved to their places, lined up in ranks and rows, and dressed down to ensure proper distancing.

"Matt," Theresa said, "I want to be over there with the crew, please." Matt dutifully pushed her to her place in front of her crew next to her XO, Lt. Brady, locked the chair's wheels, and took his place. Sophie got a chair with the families and friends of the crew seated close by. She was excited, trying her best to mind her behavior, but fidgety nonetheless. A stern look from her father reminded her to sit still. Admiral Kincaid approached the podium. He introduced all the dignitaries that were present and then began his speech. He read the unit citation aloud.

"On June 1st, 2025, Patrol Craft 15, the Derecho, was undergoing modernization and sea trials. A series of attempted ship takeovers occurred nationwide; one was successful, the LP gas carrier Frances Mahan. The apparent intent of the terrorist was to sail the Mahan to the port of New York and, once there, to detonate its cargo, causing massive injuries and death. The Derecho was sent to intercept the Mahan, despite being in a half-finished state and having an inexperienced crew.

"The Derecho materially assisted US Navy SEALs in the recapture of the Mahan, saving thousands of lives in the process. During the retaking of the Mahan, Lt. Commander Leslie was seriously injured, and several others were wounded. Lt. Terry Brady assumed command, instituting damage control efforts and successfully returning the Derecho to port.

"The officers and crew of the Derecho overcame many obstacles and successfully completed the mission assigned to them in the finest traditions of the Naval Service.

"I am proud to present this Presidential Unit Citation to the officers and men of the Derecho. Lt. Commander Leslie, will you please come forward."

Lt. Brady moved to push Theresa towards the podium. She waved him off and struggled to her feet. Using only a cane to assist her, Theresa walked slowly but steadily to the podium. She saluted Admiral Kincaid and accepted the citation on behalf of the crew.

"Thank you, sir."

As she turned to go back to her seat, Admiral Kincaid stopped her.

"About face, Commander," he said.

"Sir?"

"I'm not done yet. Standby."

"Lt. Brady, come forward."

Brady stepped smartly up to the podium, standing beside Theresa, saluted smartly, and waited.

"At the direction of the President of the United States, the following promotion is made. Lt. Commander Leslie to full Commander." Admiral Kincaid approached Theresa, handing her the document and a pair of new Commander's shoulder boards for her uniform. She smiled and saluted.

Theresa heard Sophie yelling and clapping her hands in the background. She couldn't help the smile that forced its way onto her face.

Admiral Kincaid returned to the podium. "At the direction of the President of the United States, the following promotion is made. Lt. Brady to Lt. Commander." Brady stepped forward, accepting the document and new Lt.

Commander shoulder boards. He saluted and returned to his place.

Theresa and Brady stood by Admiral Kincaid as he awarded individual medals to the crew. Theresa was delighted when each member of the crew received the "Global War on Terrorism Service Medal" (GWOTSM) and Purple Heart for those who were wounded in action. When Theresa started to tire, Brady had Matt bring her wheelchair forward so she could remain with Admiral Kincaid as her crew received their medals.

"In closing, I wish to extend my personal congratulations to the officers and men of the Derecho for a job well done."

 Everyone adjourned to a nearby tent for refreshments. Theresa and Brady were inundated with congratulations and handshakes from dignitaries, family members, and the crew. It was Sophie, though, who gained the most attention, flying through the crowd to land on Theresa's lap. Theresa almost screamed in pain, but hugged her tight.

"Can I see your boat now, Miss Theresa?"

Theresa looked at Admiral Kincaid, who smiled and nodded.

"Sure, Sophie, let's go!" Matt wheeled Theresa to the gangplank. She stood, grabbing the ropes for support. As she started to walk aboard, Brady yelled, "Bosun, man the sides!"

Theresa looked up to see six of her sailors in spotless white and a Bosun with his pipe, ready to pipe her and Sophie aboard.

Yep, Brady thinks of everything, she said to herself, smiling from ear to ear, and her eyes getting a little misty. As Theresa came aboard, she saluted the flag and the officer of the day.

Brady, Matt, and Sophie escorted her to the bridge, standing by while she let Sophie sit in the captain's chair and explained all the controls in view. Next was the captain's cabin, where Theresa relaxed in a chair while Matt showed Sophie the lower decks.

"I'm glad you are getting the Derecho, Terry. You deserve it."

"Thanks, Ma'am. I know the Derecho means a lot to you. I'll treat her right."

"I know you will. From now on, it's Theresa in private, alright?" Theresa said.

"Yes, Ma'am, I haven't heard formally, but I believe Nolan will be my new XO," Brady said, pouring her a cup of coffee before sitting opposite her.

"Good choice," Theresa said.

"How's the boat?" Theresa asked, sipping her coffee.

He even remembered how I take my coffee.

"Getting there. The minor damage has been repaired. The hole the RPG punched in the hull will be fixed shortly, so we can continue our trials. A few new crew members will replace those injured. We should be ready for the rest of our sea trials in less than a month."

"That's great, Terry. I'm happy for you."

"How about you?" Brady asked.

"Admiral's staff. With luck, I'll be teaching some."

"Sorry to hear that, ma'am. I know you'd rather be at sea. Hopefully, it won't last too long, and you'll be back on a ship."

Sophie ran into the room, overtired and ready for a nap. Matt followed.

"Do you mind, Terry?" Theresa asked.

"Of course not. The far bunk is still yours, officially. It's a good spot for a nap."

Matt lay Sophie on the bunk, and in moments, she was asleep. He snapped a picture with his cell phone camera, then walked over and sat with Brady and Theresa.

"She may not remember all of this when she gets older. I'll have this to show her. I got one when she sat in the captain's chair, too."

"What about you two?" Brady asked. "Have you figured out how to sort this out and stay together?"

"No," Theresa admitted. I looked at the regs. Our options are limited. At a minimum, we can't be assigned to the same unit."

"If you are on the Admiral's staff, that part is at least taken care of, "Brady offered.

"There's more to it than that, but yeah, it helps," Theresa said.

Brady sighed. "I hate to be the one to say it, but the only way around it is if one of you resigns your commission."

"No way," Theresa and Matt said together.

"Well, I hope you two can find a better way. Good luck." With that, Brady stood and left the cabin. Matt and Theresa were quiet, contemplating what he had said.

"There has to be another way," Theresa said finally.

Matt shook his head." No, I'm afraid he's right. The rules are convoluted, but all point to the same thing."

They sat quietly for a while, watching Sophie sleep.

Eventually, Matt looked at Theresa and said, "Therese, do you love me?"

Theresa's stomach tightened. *That's the real question, isn't it? Do I love you enough to resign my commission and become your wife?*

"Yes, Matt, I do," she replied." I want to build a life with you and Sophie."

"I love you too, Therese," Matt admitted. "I've had some job offers from a couple of major defense contractors. It would mean a stable environment for Sophie and decent pay and benefits."

"Matt, don't. We can figure this out together," Theresa pleaded.

I can't ask him to give up his career just to marry me.

"I promise I won't do anything rash without talking to you first," Matt said. "For me, the Navy has been a good career choice. For you, it's been your life. I won't ask you to sacrifice all that you've accomplished. I'll look into it and let you know."

***

A few weeks later, Theresa was released from the hospital. She had sufficiently recovered to be alone if she took it easy. She was happy to be home, lying on her own bed, holding pillows tight, and thinking of Matt. She'd talked to one of her friends in the legal section of headquarters, confiding in her the problem she and Matt had. They said they would look into it, but Brady was right. Fraternization between ranks was prohibited except under very specific circumstances.

So, what do I do? Matt's right. The Navy has been my life. I wouldn't want to do anything else. Matt has career aspirations, too. I can't let him give up everything for me.

***

Theresa sat on her patio, watching the Derecho leave port, ready to resume sea trials. She thought wistfully,

Whatever we decide, I'll never go to sea on her again. It's party gowns and cocktail napkins for me from now on— the navy's showpiece.

She looked at her watch, sighed, and stood up to begin getting ready for Admiral Kincaid's party tonight.

***

"I don't know how you do it, Margot," Theresa said. Theresa and Margot met at the beach for some girl time. They lay on the hot, white sand and baked.

"What do you mean, Therese?" Margot replied, adjusting her sunglasses. Her naturally dark skin didn't really need a suntan to look great, but the feel of the sun on her was wonderful. Her extremely small bikini reflected Margot's confident and independent outlook on life.

"My nominal position on Admiral Kincaid's staff is logistics. I'm learning a lot, but the lieutenants and NCOs really run the place. It's been three weeks, and aside from signing a few papers every day and conferences with the Admiral, all I do is talk to bigwigs about the Mahan and how the Navy needs more counterterrorism patrol boats like the Derecho, just in case. Smile and schmooze."

"Welcome to the Blue Dress Navy," Margot replied bitterly. "How do I handle it? I dress to the nines every night, mutter polite bullshit to whoever I have to dance with, and demurely decline their indecent proposals. One thing, though."

Margot rolled over to face Theresa." I didn't join the Navy to be a prostitute. Never let them touch you anywhere you don't want them to. Draw the line. They'll promise you anything to get you in bed. Take my advice. Walk away. They won't even remember your name in the morning."

"Damn, Margot. That's harsh."

"It'll happen to you sometime. Some bigwig whose wife stayed home will want a playmate. If you have any integrity, put them in their place. If all you are looking for is a quick way to a promotion, you can sleep your way to the top. It's been done before. I may never become an admiral, but when I took my husband to bed on our wedding night, it was my first time. I'm not giving it up to anyone else."

Theresa lay on her stomach, thinking.

I hate this part of Navy life: politics and horny congressman. I have to get back out to sea. I wish I could help Margot, Theresa told herself. *Hell, I can't even help myself.*

CHAPTER 3

Theresa's moment of decision came sooner than she thought. She wore her favorite blue gown, silver dangle earrings, pearls, and white high heels. She'd spent a long time at the hairdresser's that morning, and a professional makeup artist had put her makeup on. Stunning was hardly an adequate description. Admiral Kincaid had briefed her on what to say to yet another junket of Congressmen, particularly Joseph Nichols, who was on the budget and taxation committee. Theresa had dressed in her best dress uniform to deliver a short speech on the Mahan incident before changing into her blue dress backstage. Despite being introduced to many power brokers who were all assistants to the undersecretary of-whatever, she couldn't remember, the permanently affixed smile on her face hid mounting boredom. It was almost automatic by now, the fixed smile, answering the same old questions with the same rehearsed answers as if whoever asked them had thought of something original. She had tuned out of the conversation early in the evening.

After several sweaty-handed dance partners had gone by, Admiral Kincaid introduced her to "Congressman Joseph

Nichols. Congressman, this is Commander Theresa Leslie."

"A pleasure, Commander. Would you care to dance?"

Congressman Joseph Nichols was well known among the blue-dress navy. Short, balding, and overweight, even the most career-oriented female officers tried to steer clear of him.

"Congressman Nichols. A pleasure to meet you," Theresa said, following his lead onto the dance floor.

"Commander Leslie, I understand you did a great job on the seizure of the LP gas ship. I'd like to add my congratulations and well done also."

Theresa replied with a fixed, professional smile on her face. "Thank you, Congressman." However, if Nichols had looked in her eyes, he would have seen the truth. *Let's get this over with. I'd rather be helping Sophie get ready for school tomorrow. I can't wait to get these shoes off; my feet are killing me.*

Theresa answered the usual questions: "Where are you from? Why did you join the Navy? How long have you been in the Navy? Are you married? etc., etc., etc." Nichols only left out, "What are you doing after this is over?" It was the same at every event. Her answers were always the same. She hardly had to listen anymore.

Theresa felt Nichol's hand squeezing her ass. That brought her back to reality.

She was startled. She'd had to endure intimate questions and overt suggestions before, usually late in the evening as people started to leave. That, unfortunately, was part of the blue dress navy. A polite but firm no was usually enough. No one had ever been so blatant as to grab her ass in the middle of so many witnesses before. His eyes were locked onto her cleavage, making her skin crawl. Theresa firmly grasped his hand and moved it back to her waist.

"Do you like shore duty, Commander?" Nichols asked, his eyes finally on her face.

"It's OK, for now," she responded. *How long is this dance?*

"What are your career goals, Commander? May I call you Theresa? Where do you want to be this time next year?"

"Wherever the Navy sends me, congressman," Theresa replied cautiously.

"If you'd like, I can arrange for you to be detailed to my office, sort of a liaison officer with the Navy department."

I know what kind of liaison you're thinking about. No thanks.

When Theresa didn't reply, Nichols tried another angle.

"You had your own command once, a small command, but a command. Would you like to go back to sea?"

Of course, I want to get back to sea! she thought.

"Sir, I appreciate your interest in my career," Theresa said, "I'm fine, thank you."

 Nichols guided Theresa into a corner of the dance floor away from most of the spectators and then stopped dancing.

"If you did want to get back to sea, I can help you," he pressed, pulling their bodies together firmly. Theresa tried to back away, create distance between them, but he held her too tightly. Nichols began rubbing his body against hers.

Is he for real? Right here in front of all these people?

 He's offering me a sea command in exchange for sex! A way out of the blue dress navy. All I have to do is...

When the congressman's hand slipped down between her breasts, Theresa leaned forward, whispering in his ear.

"Remove your hand, or I'll break it, sir."

Nichols laughed quietly instead. "I've heard that before, Theresa, but in the end, you'll come around- if you ever want to leave this, what do you girls call it? The blue dress navy?"

Theresa recoiled as Nichol's slipped his hand further inside her dress. Though the fixed professional smile was still on her lips, she had had enough. Theresa grabbed Nichols' fingers, jerked his hand out of her gown, and shoved him to the floor. The band stopped. It was deathly quiet as people watched what was happening. They even heard the pop as Theresa broke his fingers.

Nichols screamed, yanking his hand free of hers and holding it with his other hand. It was already turning colors as the swelling began.

"I'm a Naval Officer, Congressman, not a prostitute!" Theresa thundered,

"Keep your hands to yourself!"

 One of Nichol's aides helped him off of the floor. Nichols' baleful glare promised that she had not heard the last of this. Theresa was so angry that she didn't care.

Across the room, Admiral Kincaid watched, chuckling. *I'd have paid good money to see his face when she did that. I will have to reprimand her in some fashion, but I'm damn glad to have been here to see that old pervert get his.*

Theresa stormed out of the ballroom, incensed. One of Admiral Kincaid's aides intercepted her as she got in her car.

"The Admiral wants to see you first thing in the morning, Commander."

"Get out of the way, or I'll run your ass over!" Theresa yelled, putting her car in reverse. The aide jumped out of the way just in time to miss being struck as Theresa sped away.

When Theresa parked in her driveway, she was still furious. She sat there for a moment with her head on the steering wheel, then started crying.

Is this it? After competing so hard in college and winning an appointment to the academy, only to have some asshole paw me in front of a room full of people? Look at me; I'm so powerful. I can do anything I want, and you won't say a word because you all fear me! I am supposed to stand there and take it because this lecherous old fool sits on some powerful committee and can make or break my career if I don't become his whore?

Theresa fished her house keys out of her purse and began walking to the door, sniffling and wiping tears from her eyes.

She hadn't noticed the car parked in front of her house.

Theresa shut the door behind her and began walking to the kitchen.

There's got to be a bottle of something in the refrigerator. I'm going to get drunk and try to forget this night.

"Therese? What's wrong, honey?"

Matt was standing in the living room. Theresa was initially confused, but then remembered she'd given him a house key while she was in the hospital.

Theresa rushed to his arms, hugged him, and lay her head on his shoulder. Matt had no idea what was happening; he'd thought to surprise her and take her out to dinner at one of the hideaways they'd found. He was not prepared for tears.

"What's wrong, Therese? Tell me, please," Matt said, guiding her to the couch where they could sit and talk. Theresa blurted out the whole story, her anger at being placed in such a situation, and how useless she felt being just a navy showpiece.

"I've destroyed my career. I'll never go to sea again," she said quietly. "All because I didn't let some horny old bastard feel me up."

"Hey," Matt said softly, rocking her slowly and brushing the tears from her eyes," I'm proud of you. You did the right thing. Now, I don't have to track him down and punch him out."

Theresa laughed at that, sniffled, and then asked,

" Why are you here, Matt? I thought the Derecho was at sea on a shakedown patrol?"

We were," he admitted, "but one of the engines blew up, and we had to hobble back to port. They still haven't upgraded them like they said they would."

Matt looked at Theresa closely. " Isn't this the famous blue dress your friend Margot was talking about? You look absolutely gorgeous in it. How about we go upstairs, and I take it off you?"

Therese stood up, laughing, wiping away the last of the tears. "From a lecherous old man to a lecherous young man. My luck is improving."

They walked upstairs to her bedroom together. Theresa put her jewelry in its box and turned back to Matt, feeling vulnerable and insecure. "Do you mind if we just snuggle a while instead?"

"With you? The Congressman beater? Any day of the week." Matt kicked off his shoes and lay on her bed. Theresa lay next to him, blue dress and all, feeling his strong arms holding her. Here, she felt protected, valued, and loved. Matt stroked her hair for a long while until Theresa gradually fell asleep.

She shouldn't have to deal with crap like this.

CHAPTER 4

"Admiral Kincaid will see you now, Commander Leslie," Lt. Marks, the admiral's aide, said.

"Thank you, Toby. I'm sorry about last night."

"No problem, Ma'am," He replied, opening the door for her.

Theresa was dressed in her uniform of the day, khakis with trousers. Her cover (hat) was on precisely as described in regulations, and her salute was crisp and smart. None of this would matter ultimately, but it was one less thing he could yell at her about.

Admiral Kincaid returned her salute, not bothering to stand up. "At ease, commander." He motioned to a chair," Sit down. I want to hear your version of what happened last night."

" Congressman Nichols intimated that if I ever wanted to get back to sea, I'd have to have sex with him. He had already squeezed my ass, and his fingers were going inside my dress. I told him to remove his hand. He just laughed and continued to push his hand inside my bra. I forcibly removed his hand and shoved him away. In the course of this, he was injured, sir."

"I see. Any witnesses to support your assertions?" Admiral Kincaid asked.

"Everyone on the dance floor, sir. I was mad and embarrassed by the congressman's unwanted touching, sir."

Admiral Kincaid leaned back in his chair, looking directly at Theresa." It may interest you to know that Congressman Nichols has two broken fingers, Commander. I spoke with him this morning. As you may imagine, his version of events is slightly different. You have made a very powerful enemy, Commander Leslie."

"Yes, sir," Theresa replied.

Admiral Kincaid threw a guest list for the party onto his desk in front of Theresa.

"There are a couple of ways this can go. This is a list of everyone at the party last night. File a complaint against Nichols, have it investigated, and cause a big stink in an election year for him, or accept a verbal reprimand from me for conduct unbecoming, which will never be entered in your personnel file, and accept a transfer to a different assignment that does not involve formal dress wear and parties. In all likelihood, it will be a royal pain in the ass for you. It involves travel to almost every naval base on the East Coast, speeches, and additional duties I will assign you. This is a 120-day assignment, at the end of which you will report back to me on your findings."

"Sir, what is the secondary job besides speeches and training?"

"You are to be my personal observer on the final sea trials of the Navy's small boat fleet. You will observe each ship as it goes through this final phase and talk to the crew, particularly if they have any suggestions for improvements or identify any faults that need to be addressed. Report back to me in 120 days."

"Sir, how many small boats are in the small boat fleet?" Theresa asked.

The Admiral replied, "There is only one at present, the Derecho. Before I release it to the fleet, I want to be sure it can take it. Inspect the boat from stem to stern, talk to everyone, and watch them as it goes through its final paces. If it passes, Derecho will be the first coastal defense craft the Navy has had in quite a long time. Several other boats will be purpose-built to cover both coasts and the Gulf of Mexico."

The Derecho! My old boat! I can get out of DC, get back on the water, and spend quality time with Matt. If I can write a good report on the patrol craft being reborn, Dozens of new PCs might be built. It's a useful assignment that keeps me out of Nichols' sight until everything blows over. If I don't take it, I'll be stuck in DC for years, maybe my entire career.

"Sir, can I take an assistant with me? Someone to act as my scheduler and typist?"

"I don't see why not. You'll be busy doing the work and giving lectures. Do you have anyone in mind?"

A few minutes later, Theresa left the admiral's office, trying to hide the smile on her face. Admiral Kincaid's secretary, a lieutenant named Meghan Fisher, waved to her to wait a minute. They walked into the breakroom and sat at a table.

"Commander, I want you to know something," Meghan said in a low voice.

"What's that?"

"What happened last night is all over headquarters already. For what it's worth, some of us appreciate what you did. I don't know if I'd have had the nerve."

"Thank you, Lt. Fisher," Theresa said. *It makes me feel better after I let that slime off the hook.*

"That's not all. I took the call this morning when Nichols called. I listened in when the Admiral and Nichols talked," Meghan said conspiratorially. "The admiral backed you up to the hilt, ma'am. Nichols was all bluster and threats, saying he was going to talk to the Secretary of Defense, the Navy, and anyone else it took to get you canned. Admiral Kincaid told him about the shitstorm you could start and asked how it might affect his reelection chances.

I loved it when the Admiral asked how Nichol's wife took the news of his 'injury.' She's one of those big-money people in New England. She finances him. He got everything he owns, including his seat in Congress, from her support. What would happen if the real story came to light? Ultimately, Admiral Kincaid suggested that Nichols let him handle the whole thing quietly. Nichols has more to lose than a seat in Congress if his antics get back to Momma.

"Commander, Admiral Kincaid is due another star next year. That has to go through Nichols' committee first. He put that on the line to help keep Nichols off your back."

Theresa sat back, amazed. She hadn't expected to hear that.

"Thanks, Meghan. I had no idea."

"He'd have backed you if you'd filed the complaint, Ma'am. It's the kind of man he is."

"How do you know I'm not filing a complaint, Meghan?" Theresa asked.

 Meghan just smiled.

" You were listening in, weren't you?"

Meghan shrugged," I know a lot of things, Commander. I know everything that happens in this place." Then, she stood up and returned to her desk.

Theresa stood up herself, laughing, and walked down the hall to her office. When she opened the door, she was surprised to see a huge bouquet of multicolored flowers on her desk. When she read the card, Theresa had to smile. It said,

From the Blue Dress Navy.

Thank you.

There were quite a few signatures on the card along with comments like, "I've wanted to do that myself, but I never had the courage," "You should have punched the bastard," and other such sentiments. Theresa took a picture of the flowers and promised herself to have that and the card framed and mounted on her wall.

***

"There will be a lot of driving because not all commands can give us the necessary dates. We'll hit a few, then backtrack some. I have a few civilian groups they want you to speak to, mostly retired Navy and Coasties. One or two local radio stations want you on air too, so you'd better have packed some nice stuff to wear," Margot said as she drove out of the front gate. "The admiral ok'd a car for us and per diem too, so we can live in the transiting officer's quarters when we can and a few of the less expensive alternatives outside the base if we have to. That leaves some extra bucks for fun time."

"Sounds good, Margot. I'm looking forward to blowing off some steam. Where's the first stop?"

"Massachusetts. There are three places, including one civilian group. Best I could do, sorry." Margot adjusted her sunglasses. They drove up Interstate 95 for an hour in peaceful silence before Margot spoke up.

"Theresa, I want to thank you for getting me out of that place, at least for a while."

"Who else could I pick? My best friend and fellow blue dress sailor? It was a no-brainer. You gave me some good advice when I started on the ball dress circuit. 'Don't let yourself become a prostitute,' or something like that. I couldn't even think when that asshole started pawing me. I remembered what you said, though. The rest was history."

"Guess I should pat myself on the back then, too," Margot laughed. One thing, though. When we get to Boston, I've booked us separate rooms off base."

"Why's that? I don't snore," Theresa teased.

"My husband is going to meet me in Boston. We plan to explore the sights together over the two days we are there. I hope you don't mind."

"I don't mind. Two days alone without the kids? You horny bastards aren't even going to leave the hotel room."

Margot screamed and laughed, nearly driving off the road.

Why didn't I think of that? I'll call Matt later; maybe we can work it out. Two days alone together in Boston? That sounds fantastic.

By the time they arrived in Boston, the third stop on their tour of speeches and rubber-chicken dinners with local politicians, Theresa and Margot had established an effective pattern. The hosting unit typically had an auditorium and a screen for their use. While Theresa spoke with the local brass, Margot distributed handouts to everyone in attendance. After the speech, they were invited to dinner at a reception or the unit commander's home. Margot and Theresa, veterans of the Blue Dress Navy, handled it easily.

Boston turned out to be different. Theresa met Margot's husband, Jacob, a strapping, handsome, dark-skinned man. They had arrived a day early for the presentation. Theresa politely declined their invitation to dinner and went to her room to catch up on her notes for the report due when they returned.

It's too bad Matt couldn't make it.

Sophie had a grade school play (she was a talking tree). Theresa forbade Matt to miss it and silently wished she were there.

I'm starting to get really domesticated.

You had better watch it, Sea Witch, or you'll grow a big bottom and clean the house on the weekends while he plays golf.

Theresa was sound asleep when the knocking and moaning started in the room next door. It was relatively quiet at first, but grew louder and louder.

Theresa laughed, turned on the lights, and waited.

They had better move the bed away from the wall, or they'll have to pay for the hole they make.

The banging stopped, and peace returned a few minutes later. Theresa could finally go back to sleep, wishing Matt were there and feeling a little jealous of her friend, Margot.

The next morning, Theresa was dressed, ready to head to the civic group's meeting hall for her canned speech. Margot was late. When time started getting uncomfortably short, Theresa went to her room and knocked. Jacob answered, bleary-eyed and, judging by the way he hid behind the door, naked.

"Uh, Hi. Tell Margot we have to be there in twenty minutes."

"Sure, sure. She is getting ready, I think." Theresa could see Margot's bare leg on the bed. Jacob turned and went to shake her awake, failing to close the door completely. It swung open slowly, confirming that Jacob hadn't dressed before coming to the door. Theresa turned around, laughing to herself, and quickly walked away.

"You two must have had one hell of a night last night," Theresa said as she drove to the civic hall. Margot didn't answer. She sat still, wearing a pair of dark sunglasses Jacob had given her. Theresa straightened Margot's uniform as they walked to the hall entrance.

"Are you sure you can do this, Margot?" Theresa asked, concerned that Margot would get sick or appear hungover to the crowd.

"Blue Dress Navy," Margot answered, haltingly. When they entered the hall, Margot's whole demeanor changed. The fixed smile and practiced happy attitude she reserved for public occasions shone through.

Wow. I hope she can keep it up until later this afternoon. I'll tell the base commander I feel bad, leftovers from my wounds, and take her back to the hotel. That is an Oscar-winning performance in the making.

***

The speech went as expected, with the usual questions asked and answered until the very end.

"Are there any more questions?" Theresa asked, her mind already leaving the room ahead of her. A hand rose in the back, and an elderly woman stood up.

"That was a very nice presentation, Commander. I do have one question, if you don't mind."

"Yes, ma'am, go ahead, please."

"How did Congressman Nichols break his hand? I believe you were present when it happened."

Theresa felt like she had been slapped in the face. She was totally at a loss for words.

What the hell? Who is this? How does she know?

Theresa stammered, trying to come up with a reply." Ma'am, I, uh, I'm here to talk about the Mahan incident. You'll have to, ah, contact the congressman's office on that." Theresa smiled at the crowd and waved. "Thank you, everyone, for hosting this seminar. Have a great day!" Theresa walked off stage quickly to a smattering of applause. She was feeling like she, not Margot, was going to puke and needed to find a restroom, NOW.

Margot walked in and locked the door behind her. She put her arm around Theresa, who was leaning over a sink.

"What the hell was that, Margot?" Theresa gasped. She hadn't expected to have such a strong reaction to the unexpected question.

"That," Margot said quietly, "was Rachel Nichols, Congressman Nichols' wife. She wants to talk to you."

Theresa turned around and leaned against the sink as this news sank in.

She looked questioningly at Margot. "Are you shitting me?"

This is not happening!

Margot said," She is in an office down the hall. She isn't used to waiting either, so if you are ready..."

Theresa stood up, took a few calming breaths, and nodded to her. Margot led her down the hall, opened the door to the office, and let Theresa enter first.

"Thank you, that will be all," Mrs. Nichols said dismissively. Under other circumstances, Margot would have told her to shove it up her ass, but she recognized this woman was not someone to be trifled with and withdrew. She stopped just outside the door where she could hear what was going on inside.

"Sit down, Commander," Mrs. Nichols said. Theresa knew the rotund elderly woman sitting before her, wearing clothes a decade or more out of fashion, was one of the wealthiest women in New England. *Those piercing gray eyes don't miss much, I bet.*

"You know who I am, don't you?"

"Yes, Ma'am. You're Congressman Nichols' wife." Theresa said suspiciously.

"And you are the woman my husband groped. You broke two of his fingers." She said this as a fact, not a question. Theresa nodded nervously, wondering where this was going.

"Why didn't you file a sexual molestation charge against him? There were plenty of witnesses, weren't there?" Mrs. Nichols demanded.

"Admiral Kincaid gave me the guest list and told me to if I wanted. He gave me a second choice I felt more comfortable with."

"You mean this trumped-up speaking tour and his assurance that my husband wouldn't retaliate?"

"I trust Admiral Kincaid, ma'am," Theresa said, starting to get mad.

Does this bitch think she needs to threaten me, too?

"I've known Anthony for years. He is a nice boy, but he doesn't know how devious my husband can be."

She shifted herself so she could lean forward. "I have been aware of my husband's infidelities almost since I married him thirty years ago. It's common knowledge to our friends and an embarrassment to me, but I let it go on far too long. I enjoy being a congressman's wife with all the perks and behind-the-scenes power plays. I do not intend to lose my position over this, but it is time to teach him a lesson. You have inadvertently provided me with the tool I need."

Theresa sat there quietly. She was dying to ask what Mrs. Nichols would do.

Mrs. Nichols rummaged through her purse for a moment, then handed Theresa a business card.

"These are my solicitors. If you find that Joseph has gone back on his word or retaliates against you or Anthony in any way, please let them know. I will fix his wagon."

Mrs. Nichols lurched to her feet and headed to the door.

Obviously, the audience is over. Theresa thought.

As she left, Mrs. Nichols' parting words were, "Watch the papers!"

Margot walked into the office, taking the seat Mrs. Nichols had just vacated.

"Holy shit!" was all she could say.

The rest of the tour proceeded without any new surprises, except for a brief mention in a few tabloids about the Congressman and Mrs. Nichols's trial separation and the difficulties her withholding of funds from his campaign was causing. Mrs. Nichols was reported to have said they would try to iron out their differences, but until then, she had thrown him out of her house.

She wasn't kidding. His reelection bid might collapse if she turns off the money tap for too long.

There was a sort of satisfaction in this, the congressman squirming and having to go hat in hand to mega-donors, pleading for funding, his reelection campaign on shaky ground.

***

"Welcome aboard, Commander," Lt. Commander Brady said.

"Thank you. This is my assistant, Lieutenant Margot Ritter."

"Glad to know you. Right this way, ma'am, "Brady accompanied them to the bridge.

Theresa stood there for a moment, remembering. Her first command. Her old captain's chair was a powerful magnet, drawing her in.

Theresa saw Matt at his station. They exchanged quick smiles before he returned to work.

While Brady gave commands to get underway, Margot said, "Kinda small, isn't it?"

"Yes, but full of memories," Theresa replied wistfully.

"I've never been to sea," Margot said nervously as she felt the deck's vibration under her feet. They were moving.

"Wait until we really get going. This boat can move!"

As if reading Theresa's mind, Brady said, "The engines have been overhauled and tested. Thirty-five knots is nothing!"

Margot's eyes got bigger. Her stomach was already rumbling its warning at ten knots. "Thirty-five knots!"

"In second gear, Lieutenant," Brady said proudly." Derecho can fly now!"

As they reached open water and turned towards the live fire training area, Theresa watched in amusement as Margot began succumbing to the nausea in her stomach. It had been a long time since Theresa had to worry about seasickness.

"Captain, what are we having for lunch?" Theresa said, sharing an evil smile with Brady.

"The menu is cream of potato soup or menudo, raw oysters on the half shell, deep-fried calamari, and sardines in oil, just the way you like them, ma'am."

"What's menudo?" Margot gasped, her hand over her mouth.

"Cow belly, pig's feet, and red chili pepper. It is amazing. You have to try it." Theresa said.

Margot began retching and walked quickly to the rail. "Captain, could someone escort Lt. Ritter to the head?"

Brady motioned to one of the sailors standing nearby, a grizzled old chief who favored chewing tobacco. He was well-versed in navy traditions, having crossed the equator a long time ago and having had the ritual meeting with King Neptune. He nodded and walked out to assist Margot. The Chief made sure to spit downwind of her and was rewarded with whatever remained in her stomach flying by.

"That was mean, Theresa," Brady said, grinning.

"Yeah. My first commander did that to me, Terry, as soon as we got past the breakwater. I didn't make it to the rail," Theresa laughed.

Brady put the Derecho through its paces on the way to the live fire area. On the flat, calm sea, the Derecho really did seem to fly. Theresa watched as Brady launched a practice anti-ship missile at the target ship, following up with machine gun and cannon fire that raked its deck. It brought back memories of the Mahan as the SEALs seized the ship and that awful moment when she saw the RPG streaking toward her. Margot, now fortified with medicine from the pharmacist's mate, noticed Theresa turning pale and her horrified expression. She grabbed her arm and gently shook her, breaking Theresa's train of thought.

"Where were you just now, Theresa?"

"I was back there. I saw the rocket coming towards me, and I didn't get out of the way."

"Couldn't get out of the way, Theresa. That's history. You survived, Ok?"

Margot realized Theresa was trembling. All she could do to comfort her was surreptitiously squeeze her hand.

Matt was busy at his weapons station. He saw Theresa's distress. He wanted to rush over and hold her, tell her everything was okay, but he knew he couldn't. He almost missed Brady's next firing command.

***

Before long, the boat was returning to its berth, having passed certification easily.

After they tied up, Theresa and Margot headed towards the gangplank, Brady in tow.

"You did a great job, Commander. Derecho's ready. Hopefully, she is the first of many more PCs to come."

"WE did a great job. You started preparing her for this day, taking her through combat and back. You are as much responsible as I am for the great shape she is in." Salutes were exchanged, and Brady handed Theresa a small box with a bow on top of it before she left.

"Open it later, Theresa. Thanks for everything."

As they drove away, Theresa had to open the box. Inside was a large navy coffee mug with her name and the crest of the Derecho on it. There was also a challenge coin with the ship's crest on it. Theresa smiled, a tear coming to her eye.

Yep, Brady thinks of everything.

CHAPTER 5

Two weeks later, Derecho was on its way to New York, where it would be celebrated for saving thousands of New Yorkers' lives during the annual visit of tall sailing ships from around the world.

"Matt, if you don't mind, I'd like to take Sophie out while you are away. Playgrounds, shopping, stuff like that. My sister Jackie is having a birthday party for her daughter, too. Lots of kids will be there."

Matt replied, "Sure, just coordinate with my mom. A little mommy time with you would be good for her."

Step mom. Not even that, really. Theresa reflected forlornly.

***

"Is Sophie ready, Beverly?" Sid yelled. It was the first time Theresa had been at Matt's mom's house. Her husband, Sid, was in his sixties, small and wiry with a dour disposition. He let Theresa in while they waited. The house, a brick split foyer with a deck and postage stamp size backyard, was beautifully decorated inside, almost as if someone had staged it for a prospective buyer. That is, until they got to Sophie's room. The floor was covered with dolls and other toys. Clothes were strewn all over the floor and bed. Coloring books and crayons were mixed in the mess. A plastic kitchen was set up in one corner where Sophie and her invisible friend, Zelda, played house. "In a minute!" Beverly replied.

Sid and Theresa walked out to the living room. He motioned to the couch, an invitation to sit, she guessed, and sat in a lounger across from her.

They stared at each other in awkward silence. Sid filled his pipe and lit it, clouding the living room with a haze of smoke as he puffed.

"So, you're Matt's girlfriend," Sid stated flatly.

"Yes. We met at the beach one day." Theresa replied, smiling warmly.

"You're older than Matt," he observed.

"Not quite two years."

"Annie was a year younger than Matt," Sid remarked sourly.

Theresa blinked. *What an odd thing to say.*

"You outrank him, too, I believe." Sid continued, his eyes looking right through her. "I was a Chief. Took me years to get there. There weren't many women officers then. None in submarines."

Where's he going with this? Theresa wondered uneasily.

"Chiefs run the Navy, always have." Sid declared, pointing his pipe at Theresa as if daring her to contradict him.

"Shut up, Sid!" Beverly declared as she and Sophie walked into the living room.

"Miss Theresa!" Sophie squealed, crawling into her lap and hugging her around the neck.

"Oof! How's my big girl today?" Theresa asked, relieved that the uncomfortable questioning had ended.

"I'm fine! We are going to a party!" Sophie said with delight on her face.

Theresa's sister and her husband were having a birthday party for their daughter, Julie. Lots of kids Sophie's age would be there.

"Uh-huh, you ready?" Theresa asked.

Sophie nodded vigorously and jumped down, heading for the door, dragging Theresa behind by the hand.

Sid said, "Sophie's bedtime is eight o'clock."

"Ok, I'll have her back around then," Theresa answered. *What is his problem?*

"I'll walk you out, Theresa," Beverly said.

On the way to the car, Beverly spoke. "I'm sorry, Theresa. I should have warned you. Sid was forced to retire shy of twenty years in subs, thanks to a heart condition. He's been bitter about it ever since."

"It's not just that, though," Theresa remarked, opening the car door for Sophie and ensuring she put her seatbelt on.

Beverly nodded. "He's 'Old School.' He doesn't think females should be in the Navy."

So that's it.

"I see."

Theresa was putting the keys in the ignition when Beverly leaned on the door and said, "Don't worry too much about it. Sophie is the apple of his eye. When he sees how happy you, Matt, and Sophie are, he'll come around."

"Thanks. My sister has a moon bounce and other stuff. Sophie will have a lot of fun. Be back in a few hours."

"See you then." Beverly waved as they drove off.

***

As Theresa and Sophie arrived, the party was in full swing. Kids ran wild across the backyard, falling off swings and slides and bouncing in the moon bounce.

Sophie looked at Theresa with glee in her eyes.

"Go..." Theresa started. Sophie dropped the present and ran to join the fun. " On..." Theresa laughed, picked up the present, and walked over to her sister's table.

"Hi, Jackie!"

Jackie was about Theresa's age, but a baby and the challenges of motherhood had added weight to her otherwise similar frame. Her husband, Ted, was flipping hamburgers on the grill and holding court with some of the other kids' parents. The volume of screaming and crying kids didn't faze them a bit.

"Theresa! There are wine coolers in the ice chest. The harder stuff is inside."

Theresa grabbed a bottle at random from the ice chest and sat down in the lawn chair beside Jackie.

"Ted has been trying to get everyone to do shots with him. He says it's moonshine. I tried one; it tasted like gasoline to me!"

"Thanks for the warning," Theresa said, grinning.

They sat back, watching the chaos for a while. Theresa tried to keep track of Sophie, but it was difficult at best with this many kids running in all directions.

"Where's Julie?" Theresa asked.

"Over behind the moon bounce, I think," Jackie said casually.

"How can you tell?"

"Mommy radar," Jackie replied. "Relax. If someone gets hurt, you'll know. How's the new boyfriend?"

"Matt's in New York for the week. I met his dad today."

"How did that go?"

"He's a retired chief who doesn't think women should be in the Navy, "Theresa replied.

"That bad, huh?" Jackie said, then yelled, "Robert! Stop hitting Maria with that bat, or it's time out!" Robert threw the wiffleball bat down, sulked a moment, then ran off to do something else.

"Beverly, his mom, is fine," Theresa said.

Where did Sophie go? Theresa was starting to get worried.

Theresa was about to get up and find her when Sophie came down the sliding board head first, her party dress askew. She landed in the dirt, laughed, and ran off.

"So, has Matt proposed yet?" Jackie inquired, pointing to another kid," Put Marjorie down. Robert, I swear..."

Robert's dad left the conclave at the grill and grabbed his arm. He spoke to Robert in very definite tones and made him sit on a lawn chair while the others played. No amount of crying affected the outcome.

"Not yet. We sort of have an understanding."

"Uh-huh. 'Shack up but don't pack up', right?" Jackie teased.

"It's a lot more complicated than that," Theresa said, swatting a very annoying fly away from her face.

"Is it?" Jackie said, not convinced.

"Burgers are ready. Hot dogs if you want them!" Ted yelled.

"Before you give your heart away, sis, make sure he won't break it," Jackie said.

"How did you know Ted was the one?" Theresa asked, surreptitiously stealing a potato chip from Jackie's plate.

"You know me, Theresa. I was born wild and ran with a hard crowd. Ted was the first man I'd ever met who could slow me down enough to make me want to, I don't know, think about the future. We just fit together so well. I never wanted to look at another man after I met Ted.

"Marriage isn't easy, Theresa. You can't just live on happiness and rainbows. The lust dies down after a while. We have arguments, usually about money or some stupid thing that happens. You learn about each other's bad habits, sore spots, and all the rest. If you can love someone despite all that, you can make it work."

Theresa leaned back, reaching into the cooler for another drink. She brought out a Mason jar filled with clear liquid.

"That's Ted's moonshine. Remember, I warned you," Jackie said. Theresa poured some into their glasses and returned the jar to the cooler.

She's right. It does smell like gasoline.

"I know it's going to be difficult at times, Jack. We also have to think about what's best for Sophie. Matt's woken up something that's been dormant inside me for my entire adult life. I love the Navy, and so does he. I never thought about doing anything else. Now that I've tasted what life could be, I want more. We can have it all if we can find a way around the marriage regulations."

Jackie held her glass up," Therese, I wish you and Matt all the best."

"To the Leslie sisters," Theresa said, clinking her plastic cup with Jackie's before downing the shot in one swallow.

"OH, MY GOD! That's brutal!" Theresa said, choking and laughing at the same time.

A swarm of kids congregated around the grill, each with a hamburger or hot dog bun on a plate. A table full of condiments, salads, and chips was next to it. Soon, the picnic tables were filled with hungry kids, momentarily subdued as they ate. Theresa caught Sophie's eye for a moment. Sophie smiled and continued talking to Julie, who was sitting beside her. Theresa was eating a plain hamburger, no bun, and whatever she could cobble together to represent a salad when she heard Sophie yell, "She is so real!"

Theresa looked up to see Sophie walking towards her, crying her eyes out.

"What happened, Sophie? What's wrong?" Theresa picked her up and held her in her lap, drying her tears with a napkin.

"Julie said Zelda isn't real!"

"That's because she can't see Zelda. Only you can, right?" Theresa said gently.

"Yeah," Sophie sobbed.

"Zelda is your special friend, not Julie's. Don't worry if someone says she isn't real. You know she is, OK?"

Sophie nodded, drying her tears before Theresa sent her back to finish eating.

"Not bad, for an amateur," Jackie pronounced.

There was cake and ice cream, then a piñata, and finally, the gifts were opened. When the party ended, it was getting towards evening.

"Say goodbye to Miss Jackie and Mr. Ted, Sophie."

"Bye!" Sophie said, rubbing her eyes.

"Come back anytime, Sophie!" Jackie exclaimed.

Hugs were exchanged, and soon, Theresa and Sophie were motoring back to Matt's parents' house.

"Did you have fun, Sophie? I bet you made a lot of new friends," Theresa said. When Sophie didn't reply, Theresa looked at her. Sophie had her head against the door, sound asleep.

***

"Commander Leslie, "Theresa answered as her phone buzzed. She was neck-deep in paperwork, correcting an obvious error that had a ripple effect throughout the supply chain.

How does shit like this get by procurement? "We didn't order it because blah, blah, blah. Sorry. It will take weeks to get the ISN back in the system. We'll let you know." I've got to find replacement parts before the Admiral finds out.

"Hi, Theresa, it's Beverly."

Theresa was immediately concerned. *Did something happen to Matt that I didn't hear about?*

"Hi, Bev, what's up?" *She sounds worried.*

"I'm on the way to the hospital. Sid is having angina, and the medicine isn't helping much."

Theresa was alarmed, hearing a siren in the background. "Is he ok?"

Beverly replied," I don't know, Theresa. The paramedics are just leaving. I hate to ask you, but I don't have anyone to turn to with Matt away. Could you meet Sophie at the bus stop and take her home for a while?"

"Absolutely. What time? Where does the bus stop?" Theresa grabbed a pen and a scrap of paper.

"Two o'clock, in front of our house. Thank you, Theresa. I'll let you know as soon as I know anything." Beverly rang off before Theresa remembered she had a meeting at fifteen hundred hours (3 pm).

Shit! How can I do this? I have to leave now, or I won't be at the bus stop on time. My sister is too far away. Damn it. Theresa thought for a moment.

If Sophie has a house key, we can get her some coloring books and crayons. She can sit at my desk while I'm at the meeting.

She stopped at Meghan's desk on the way out. "Could you tell the admiral I have to leave for an hour, but I'll be back in time for the meeting?"

"Yes, Ma'am. I'll tell him."

Theresa was parked in front of Matt's parents' house, looking impatiently at her watch every few minutes.

Come on! I have thirty minutes to be at the meeting!

She watched as the bus approached, stopping at almost every driveway so its young passengers didn't have far to walk. Finally, Sophie got off, waved at her friends, and began walking toward the house, her backpack slung over her shoulder.

"Sophie! Sophie, it's Miss Theresa!" Theresa got out of her car and waved. Sophie waved back and ran to her.

"Hi, Miss Theresa!" She yelled, grabbing Theresa around her waist in a tight hug.

Twenty minutes!

"Ah, Sophie, Grandmom asked if I could pick you up and take you home with me for a while. Would you like that?"

"Grandpop meets me at the bus stop every day. Is something wrong?"

Perceptive kid.

"Grandmom had to take him to the doctors. Hop in. I have to stop by work for a little while, but then you can come home with me for dinner."

Theresa raced back to the base, parked, and frog-stepped Sophie upstairs. She got Sophie a soda and sat her behind her desk with some blank paper and colored pens.

"I have to go into a meeting for an hour right over there," Theresa pointed. "Promise you will sit here and behave, OK?"

"OK, Miss Theresa," Sophie said as Theresa grabbed her laptop and started for the door. She almost collided with Admiral Kincaid in the hallway.

"Sorry, Admiral," Theresa said, stopping at the last moment. He looked over her shoulder and saw Sophie busy scribbling.

"Who do we have here?" Admiral Kincaid said, pushing past Theresa and going into her office.

"I'm Sophie!" she said, stopping her scribbling and smiling at the admiral.

"Hi, Sophie! I'm Admiral Kincaid. What are you drawing?" he said, looking over her shoulder.

Theresa felt like she was the one having a heart attack.

"A dragon!" Sophie replied, returning to her work.

Admiral Kincaid said," I see. Blue fire coming from its mouth? Must be a special dragon."

He looked at Theresa, who was nervously looking at her watch. "Relax, Commander. They can't start the meeting without me."

"Miss Theresa is Daddy's girlfriend!" Sophie said, not looking up from her coloring.

"Oh, she is? Do I know your father, Sophie?"

Theresa caught her breath. *If Sophie spills the beans...*

"Sir, the teleconference with DC is waiting," his secretary, Meghan, said, walking by.

"Very well. Carry on, Miss Sophie," the Admiral said. As he walked toward the conference room door, Theresa said, "I'm sorry, Admiral. It was an emergency."

"That's all right. She reminds me of my own grandchild."

Once the conference started, Theresa took a few minutes to settle down. She had to resist the urge to check on Sophie. Finally, it was her turn to speak.

"I spoke to Procurement this morning. There was a SNAFU. The part we need is not in stock, and none are on order. It will be a few weeks before they can order more."

"What do you suggest we do until then, Commander?" someone asked over the communications link. Theresa was about to reply when she saw the conference room door slowly open, and Sophie walked in. She went straight to Theresa, tugging on her shirt. Everyone's eyes were on Sophie.

"Uh, we can ask other commands if they have the spare parts for now, or we can scavenge used parts from the destroyer Leonard at the ready fleet dock in Newport News. "

"Miss Theresa, I have to go to the bathroom," Sophie said loudly. Everyone in the room burst into laughter. Theresa, face reddening, grabbed Sophie's hand and escorted her out.

"Five-minute break," Admiral Kincaid said, laughing.

***

For the next three days, Theresa discovered what it would be like to be a naval commander and a mom.

"Sid's doing fine, but the doctors won't let him go until they are sure," Beverly said.

Theresa responded, " At least he is stable. You keep him comfortable; I'll take care of Sophie."

"I know it's an imposition, Theresa, but ..."

"It's no imposition. I'm happy to do it. Admiral Kincaid is allowing me to flex my schedule a little until things return to normal."

For Theresa, her orderly, disciplined life became a shambles. She worked all day, picking up Sophie, taking her home, feeding and bathing her, and ensuring she and Zelda were tucked into bed. She took whatever work she could home and kept going until midnight. In the morning, she saw Sophie off to school and went to work. It was exhausting.

"Sophie's doing fine. Matt," Theresa said over the computer link. "We are getting a lot more time together until your dad comes home. I can even color inside the lines, most of the time." Matt laughed when she told him about Sophie interrupting the meeting.

"Parenting has its moments! "he said.

On the third day, Theresa received another call from Beverly. Sophie's school called. She was sick. Could you get her? Theresa took half a day off and went to the school.

I'm glad Matt thought to put me on Sophie's pickup list.

"It seems like she picked up a stomach flu that's been going around the school. "Give her some Pedialyte every few hours," the school nurse said," a cold cloth on her head, and children's aspirin. Other than that, you'll have to ride it out for the next couple of days."

Theresa took Sophie by the hand and walked her to the car. They stopped at a drug store to get what they needed, then went directly to Theresa's house. Sophie was tucked into bed, a bucket on the floor in case she got sick, a small glass of juice on the nightstand, and some of the toys Sophie had "given" Theresa littered the floor around her.

"Bev," Theresa said on the phone. "Can you watch Sophie in the morning until I get home? I can't keep missing work."

Bev agreed," Sid is doing ok right now. If he has no problems, they might let him go home Saturday or Sunday."

"Thanks, Bev. I don't know how you do it."

"Experience. Being retired helps. Matt says he wishes he were there, but his boat is on maneuvers with the Canadians somewhere near Nova Scotia."

"I know how that is. Hope he brought his long johns," Theresa laughed, leaning back against the couch." See you tomorrow morning. Bye."

I'll get my uniform ready for tomorrow, so I can go to work as soon as I drop Sophie off at Bev's in the morning.

The sound of Sophie vomiting and crying woke Theresa up. She'd fallen asleep on the couch. She grabbed a couple of dish towels and went to check on her.

The smell of vomit in the room made Theresa want to gag. She sat down on the bed and felt Sophie's head. Still warm. She held Sophie and rocked her.

"I want my daddy," Sophie cried, tears and snot running down her face. Theresa wiped Sophie's face with a cloth.

"Daddy's not here, baby. He's at sea on his boat." Theresa said soothingly.

"Where's Grandma?" Sophie whimpered, holding her doll closely.

"She's at the hospital with Grandpop. You'll see her tomorrow morning. You're staying with me tonight, ok, honey?" Cuddling Sophie and brushing her hair away from her face.

"You're not my mommy! I want my mommy!" Sophie cried, almost breaking Theresa's heart.

"I know, sweetheart, I know." Theresa hugged Sophie, stroking her head tenderly and crying right along with her until they both fell asleep.

***

Beverly unlocked the front door and yelled, "Theresa? Sophie?" She knocked again, but there was no answer. She and Sid walked in to look for them. They each checked the bedrooms.

"Over here, Bev," Sid said quietly, motioning for her. They looked in together, seeing Sophie cuddled up on Theresa's chest, both sound asleep, Theresa's arm around Sophie. Beverly smiled, and for once, Sid did, too. Beverly gently checked Sophie's forehead before patting Theresa's arm.

"Theresa," she repeated. Theresa's eyes slowly opened. "Bev? Sid? What are you doing here?"

"They let Sid go late last night, so I took him home. You'd better get moving; it's almost seven o'clock."

Theresa sat up groggily. "Oh, that's okay, thanks. Sophie's temperature broke last night. I was going to keep her home today anyway. She hasn't eaten much."

"You go get ready for work. We'll watch her until she wakes up." Sid said.

"You ok, Sid?" Theresa asked, finally getting herself untangled from Sophie.

Sid nodded. "Can't keep me in bed that long," he pronounced.

They heard the shower in Theresa's room turning off almost as soon as it came on. A moment later, it came on again for a few seconds.

A Navy shower, Sid thought in grudging approval.

"Did you hear her, Sid? She said '<u>I</u> was going to keep Sophie home today," Beverly commented.

"Yeah, so?" Sid replied.

"You can be so thick sometimes, Sid," Beverly replied. *She's becoming a mother.*

CHAPTER 6

One of the things Theresa resented the most was having to hide her relationship with Matt. She knew when he was supposed to return, but she couldn't greet him like other sailors' wives and girlfriends did. They had to sneak around to out-of-the-way places, much like they were having an illicit affair with someone else's spouse. They couldn't go to parties, shop, or do anything else locally because they feared someone they knew would see them. Theresa refused to go to a motel for the night, even with Matt. It felt dirty and cheap.

***

"This place is nice, Matt," Theresa said. They'd driven forty-five minutes to a restaurant specializing in an old-time atmosphere. Dinner and a dance floor. Waiters in suits and ties, cigarette girls, the works. A live band was playing soft music for dancing. Its clientele was usually much older than Theresa and Matt. It was a step back in time.

"First class, for my lady," Matt said. He didn't much like wearing a suit to dinner. Until he met Theresa, he'd sat in front of the TV with Sophie and eaten, using the coffee table for their dinner table. Tonight was different.

Theresa wore a lovely dress, jewelry, and stiletto heels. Their steaks were perfect, and the potatoes and green beans were lightly spiced. Matt's phone rang when they sat with their coffee, enjoying their time together. Several other guests looked at him in annoyance. Matt silenced it immediately. "I'll step outside. If you're having dessert, make it two."

Theresa watched the people swaying on the dance floor, idly wondering if Matt could slow dance, when she saw a couple leaving the dance floor that she recognized. The captain in charge of logistics at the base, and his wife. She dealt with him practically every day.

He'll recognize me immediately if he keeps coming this way.

Theresa looked around. Matt was walking back towards their table.

Shit!

The captain stopped to chat with someone at a table near the dance floor, giving Theresa a few more minutes to think.

If I can make it to the ladies' room, I'll hide there until they leave.

Theresa rose slowly to avoid attracting attention, then made her way to the powder room. Fortunately, the captain was engrossed in his conversation and didn't see her walk by.

Matt returned to their table, sat, and waited for Theresa. When she didn't return in a few minutes, he began to worry.

"Anything else you and the lady would like, sir?" the waiter asked.

"Uh, no, just the check, please," Matt said. Matt looked at the check, gave the waiter his credit card, and waited as the waiter ran it through the computer. Matt's phone rang again, drawing stares from people who didn't want their old-time atmosphere interrupted by a modern cell phone. Again. It was Theresa.

"Matt, I'm in the ladies' room."

"Anything wrong?" Matt inquired, ignoring the people at the next table.

"Is the older man in the gray suit still talking to someone a few tables over from us?"

Matt looked. "Yeah, him and his wife."

"He's a captain in the base logistics section. If he sees me, he's bound to recognize me."

"So? What's the problem?" Matt inquired, shifting his chair to look for Theresa.

"The problem is he is nosey as hell and doesn't know when to shut up."

"Oh, I see. I'm taking care of the check; meet me at the car, ok?" Matt signed the receipt and handed it back to the waiter.

"Thanks, Matt."

Matt and Theresa drove in silence for a while until Theresa couldn't stand it anymore.

"Sneaking out of the restaurant was humiliating."

"Couldn't you just tell him I was a civilian friend? He wouldn't know the difference," Matt said, trying to be helpful.

"What if he knew you from somewhere, or you two met later in uniform? It would be awkward to say the least."

Matt could tell Theresa was feeling frustrated. All the sneaking around was getting to him as well.

"Next time, just tell him I'm a gigolo you picked up at the beach. I'll open my shirt down to my belly button and wear a gold necklace and some rings."

Theresa looked at him sourly. "It's not funny, Matt. We both have a lot to lose if our relationship gets to the wrong ears."

"I know, honey," Matt said, "We have to face the fact that the longer this problem is unresolved, the higher the probability is that someone we know will see us together."

***

This time, things will be different.

Theresa had discovered a beautiful rental cabin with its own pond and pier. It was in the woods, miles away from anyone else. It would be perfect for the four-day weekend she had in mind—just her and Matt.

They arrived late Thursday night. The car had been packed and ready to go ahead of time, so after settling Sophie in with Grandma and Grandpa, they were off. The driveway to the cabin was hard to see in the dark, so even with the aid of GPS, they missed it at first.

"It's the dirt road, Matt," Theresa said, indicating a gap in the bushes. He turned in, following the rutted path. The long, dark driveway enhanced their feeling of solitude. Eventually, the headlights fell on the darkened cabin.

"Nice," Matt said as he parked. He opened the cabin door so Theresa could begin unloading the car. He took the flashlight from the glovebox and searched for the main power switch. She was dragging their cooler through the door when the lights came on.

"Found it!" She could hear Matt yelling up the basement steps.

The cabin had a well-used, rustic appearance. The furniture in the living area was overstuffed and comfortable. In the center of the main room hung a wagon wheel chandelier, with light bulbs replacing candles around the edge. The kitchen had all the modern conveniences. A note on the refrigerator stated that it took three hours or more to cool down and even longer to make ice. It was humming along as the compressor started its work.

"At least we can have coffee or tea. Want some?" Theresa asked, pouring bottled water into the Keurig machine.

"Tea, please, decaf. I want to sleep tonight."

We'll see about that, Theresa thought, a grin on her face.

This is going to be perfect—just the two of us for four solid days: jeans and plaid shirts, no uniforms. The phone is only for emergencies. The TV stays off. I should light a fire to warm the place up before we go to bed, though.

While the machine made all the groaning and squirting noises a Keurig makes while it brewed their tea, Theresa opened the flue on the fireplace and got a fire going. Soon, it was blazing away, thanks to the dry wood the owners had thoughtfully provided.

Theresa brought a mug of tea out on the deck for Matt. It was the beginning of fall: warm days and cool nights.

Snuggling weather, she mused.

"Thank you, Ma'am," Matt said, accepting a mug from Theresa. Steam rose from it, mixing with the cold air.

Theresa nestled up to him, putting her feet on the swing cushion." You can call me Therese, honey, sweetie, or even darling, but if you call me Ma'am once more, I'm going to beat you."

"Promises, promises," Matt replied. He looked around at the soft light from the house playing off the pond and listened to the whisper of the breeze through the forest. "This place is all you said it would be. Maybe next summer, we can bring Sophie and Julie up here."

"There is a spare bedroom," Theresa agreed.

Matt and Theresa stayed on the porch, watching the vast field of stars above them in agreeable silence. In a little while, he realized Theresa had fallen asleep, her soft, rhythmic breathing warming his shoulder.

"My sweet Theresa," he said softly, caressing her hair. "I never thought I could love again so deeply after Annie died. You mean the world to me."

He picked Theresa up, her head on his shoulder, and carried her to their bedroom.

***

The sun coming through the curtains woke Theresa up early. Her head rested on Matt's shoulder while she watched his muscular chest move up and down with each breath.

Handsome, gentle, and all to myself for the next three days.

I could sure get used to this.

Theresa regretfully separated herself, heading for the bathroom. The cabin was cold. She found the thermostat and set it to seventy degrees before rushing back to bed. She quickly undressed, putting on her nightshirt before slipping back into bed and cuddling with Matt.

This is where I belong, she thought as she drifted back to sleep.

***

Is she trying to drive me nuts? Matt thought. *That nightshirt barely covers anything.*

Theresa padded around the kitchen barefoot, ostensibly oblivious to Matt's eyes following her. She grinned as she bent over to get the milk from the cooler, knowing Matt was watching.

"Eggs and sausage or cereal, Matt," Theresa said.

"How about you first?" He said with a leer.

"Patience, Matt. Not on an empty stomach," she teased.

"Eggs and sausage, then."

Breakfast was on the porch. A blanket on her legs and one of Matt's flannel shirts draped over her shoulders helped. It was a little cool out, but Theresa didn't mind.

"So, what do you want to do today? "Matt asked.

"Well, while you do the dishes, I'm going to swim a bit, then bake in the sun if it gets warm enough."

"In that case, I shall finish my duties rapidly and join you," Matt replied.

Coffee and cuddling for the next few hours made the morning enjoyable. No serious topics allowed. They watched deer walk out of the woods, leisurely drinking from the pond. Formations of Canadian geese flew over, their noisy cawing fading into the distance.

"I really needed this," Matt sighed. "I love Sophie to the ends of the earth, but quiet, unhurried times like this recharge my batteries."

"I know what you mean. All the papers, conferences, and SNAFUs to sort out just wear me down."

"At least you don't have to wear that blue dress anymore," Matt said slyly.

"True," Theresa laughed. "I haven't heard a word from that jerk since I broke his fingers."

"Everyone knows only I can paw you like that!" Matt said with a straight face.

Theresa looked at him, grinned, and kissed Matt gently.” “Try it before you get those dishes done, mister,” she said, shaking her fist in front of his face.

Matt recoiled in mock horror. " OK, I'm moving.” Matt stood up to go inside. Theresa gathered the coffee mugs and silverware and started towards the sliding doors. Matt reappeared as she neared.

“Of course, you can pound on me later if you want to.” He ducked out of the way as she faked throwing a mug at him.

As Matt scrubbed a pan, Theresa went into their bedroom and emerged a moment later wearing a silver one-piece swimsuit. She was tying her hair back with a hair tie when Matt spoke.

“No.”

Theresa stopped, uncertain what he meant.

” Go back and put that bikini on you had the day we met, please.”

Theresa was obviously uncomfortable.” Matt, I can't wear things like that anymore. My scars...”

“I know all about your scars,” Matt insisted,” I was there. You earned those. Don't let anyone say otherwise.”

Theresa looked down, feeling vulnerable, “Matt, it's just that I'm sensitive about them. They're ugly.”

Matt put the wash towel down and walked over to her, putting his arms around her waist. "You are a very beautiful woman, Theresa, scars or no scars. I want YOU, not some glamour shot pin-up airbrushed to perfection. What you do anywhere else is up to you, but here, you don't have to cover up for me, okay?"

Theresa nodded, kissing Matt and hugging him tight. A tear streaked down her cheek. "Thank you. I love you, Matt Chapman," she whispered softly.

She turned and walked towards the bedroom, but stopped at the door. She turned again and looked at him.

" I didn't bring it, Matt."

"I saw you packing that one piece. I snatched the bikini off your dresser. Look in my suitcase."

She smiled and then disappeared into the bedroom.

***

Theresa dove into the pond off the dock. The water was cold but invigorating. She swam around at random until she began to tire, finally pulling herself up on the float in the center of the pond and closing her eyes. The sun was warm and got hotter the longer she lay there.

Matt stood by the porch door, drying the last of the dishes and watching Theresa swim. He couldn't help the smile that grew on his face.

Moments like these make special memories.

 He finished the last dish, placing it in the rack, then walked into the bedroom to change into his bathing suit.

I'll wait until we head back before I tell her.

***

Theresa heard the splash of water as Matt pulled himself up onto the raft.

 He looks like one of those sexy models that make women swoon in those ads.

Matt kissed Theresa before lying beside her. They lay in agreeable silence, delighting in each other's nearness. Theresa was dozing off when she felt him slowly untying her bikini top. She opened an eye to see Matt on his elbow beside her, slowly pulling the string. She felt the knot release, freeing her chest. He moved the top out of the way and then began softly nuzzling her breast. Theresa closed her eyelid again, enjoying his touch, a slight smile curving on her lips. Her mind cleared of any conscious thought as she put her arms around his head, moaning loudly as her body responded. Theresa lifted her hips so Matt could remove the last of her bathing suit. She lay naked on the float, caressing Matt's head as his gentle touch drove her wild with desire.

"Matt... Matt, please," she gasped, pulling him on top of her and pushing his swimsuit down as far as she could.

Her screams of ecstasy echoed through the woods, her fingernails raking his back.

They lay together, savoring the sensation of their bodies being joined. Matt lay his head on her shoulder, nuzzling her ear. His weight felt good on top of her. Theresa's heart was bathed in joy, the afterglow of their lovemaking. She gently ran her hands over his back and wrapped her legs around him.

This is the way it should be all the time.

***

On Saturday, Matt and Theresa decided to take a long walk around the pond. They talked about inconsequential things. Matt stopped halfway around the pond. Theresa was curious when Matt sat on a stump.

"Theresa, come sit with me."

She sat on his lap, putting her arm around his neck, and waited.

"Theresa, I love you. I know nothing about our relationship is normal, and there have been many obstacles we have had to face. Nevertheless, I know we are meant for each other." Matt reached into his pocket and pulled out a small box.

"I want to marry you, no matter what we have to overcome to do it." He opened the box. Inside was a gold engagement ring with diamonds studded around a larger central diamond.

Theresa was stunned. She looked at the ring, her heart swelling. "I love you, too, Matt. I'd marry you tomorrow if I could, but..."

"No buts, Therese." Matt looked Theresa in the eyes and kissed her hand, slipping the ring on her finger. It looked so right there.

"I talked with Base Legal a long time ago. All I was waiting for was for the job offer to be finalized and for my transfer to the Naval Reserve to be approved. After this last deployment, the way is clear for us to marry.

"Just say yes, and our dreams will come true."

Theresa couldn't believe her ears. *After all the sneaking about and drama, are we going to be married?*

"Matt, your career..." She protested.

"I will still have a career, Therese, only in the reserves. I serve a few weeks at sea once a year, and Sophie will have a stable home. You can still have a career, too. I know how hard it was to get where you are now. I'd never ask you to give that up. It won't be all peaches and cream, but we will work it out. All you have to do is say yes."

There must be a hundred things that...

"Matt, I do love you. I want to marry you right here and now. You are sacrificing a lot to make this work."

Theresa put her arms around his neck and kissed him.

"Of course, I'll marry you. Can we agree that, until all this is a reality, we don't mention it to anyone?"

"Absolutely. A few months from now, it won't matter anymore. "

Theresa's heart swelled with love as she looked at the ring. *Can this really be true, or am I dreaming?*

***

Sunday. The weekend had gone by so fast: romantic dinners, long walks through the woods, staying up late, and cuddling long into the morning hours. Standing on the dock, holding each other, watching the sun go down. Matt and Theresa's bond grew closer, stronger than ever before.

Matt had gone outside to gather more wood so they could have one last fire before leaving the next morning. He dropped half of it while trying to get back inside the cabin, but soon, the fire was blazing. Theresa emerged from the bathroom, wrapped in her long, white terrycloth robe, towel-drying her hair. She walked over to the fire, warming herself as he watched.

When her hair was dry enough, Theresa took a brush from her robe pocket. Before she could start, Matt took the brush, pulled a hassock in front of the couch, and motioned for her to sit. He began brushing her hair in long, slow strokes.

"Mmm. I love the personal service in this place," Theresa said dreamily.

When he was finished, Matt kissed her on the neck, then moved to the couch. Theresa joined him, snuggling close.

Sometimes, simple pleasures are the best, Matt reminisced as they lay together on the couch.

Sophie loves her, my mom is thrilled, and Dad will come around eventually. Life together is going to be fantastic.

The warmth of the fire, Matt's being so close, and the thought that, in a very short while, they would be a real couple, not hiding or dodging anyone, made her happier than she had ever been before.

*****

The long romantic weekend had to come to an end eventually. The drive home was bittersweet.

Secretly engaged- can you beat that! Theresa thought. *The next few weeks will be difficult, but then- Mrs. Matt Chapman!*

Theresa dropped Matt off at his apartment and then drove home.

Not for much longer! She smiled.

***

Matt and Theresa quietly began planning their wedding. Nothing was set in stone, of course, just vague ideas of where they'd live so Sophie could stay in the same school, lists of who they would invite, and the honeymoon (they agreed to take Sophie so she'd feel included in their lives). Who would likely be the best man, maid of honor, and any other details they could conceive. A military wedding would be beautiful. At this stage, it was mostly dreaming. They had time to figure it out.

***

Theresa began spending nights at Matt's apartment, knowing Sophie would wake them up sometime in the morning. They knew they couldn't trust a five-year-old ("almost six, Dad!") girl to keep their engagement secret, but they wanted her to get used to them sleeping together. That first morning, Sophie walked into her dad's room and saw Miss Theresa sleeping in bed beside him. Curious, she walked over to her father and pulled on his T-shirt sleeve. Matt opened his eyes and smiled at her.

"Dad, why is Miss Theresa sleeping in your bed?" Her curiosity required an answer.

Matt sat up, patting the bed next to him.

"Princess, that's a good question. Why don't you climb up here so the three of us can talk?"

Sophie climbed over Matt, depositing herself between him and Theresa. She looked at Theresa inquisitively.

"Good morning, Sophie," Theresa said brightly as she sat up.

"Hi, Miss Theresa. Why are you in Daddy's bed?"

That's a loaded question. She is too young to learn the answer to that one yet.

"Daddy and I wanted to talk to you this morning. You don't mind, do you?" Theresa asked.

Sophie shook her head and waited.

Here goes, Theresa thought, "Daddy and I love each other. Do you know what that means?"

"Uh-huh," Sophie replied.

"We are thinking about living together soon. Would you mind?"

"No," Sophie replied.

"Would you mind sleeping at my house when Daddy is there?"

"Can I bring some toys?" Sophie asked.

Theresa replied," Absolutely. You and Zelda can have your own room."

"I don't mind then," Sophie said.

Matt spoke up, caressing Sophie's hair. "Sophie, you know I loved your mommy and always will." He picked Sophie up and squeezed her, sitting her on his lap." She gave me you. Miss Theresa will be your stepmom one day, Ok?"

Sophie smiled, "Ok!" She crawled over to Theresa and hugged her around the neck.

Theresa's emotions swelled, threatening a cloudburst of tears. She put her arms around Sophie and kissed her cheek. "I love you too, Soph. You're one amazing little girl."

Now that Sophie had accepted Theresa being there for her and her dad most of the time, they quickly established a daily pattern. Sophie usually woke them up in the morning, and either Theresa or Matt made breakfast. They both saw her off to school. Theresa still took her morning run, but a little later. By the time she returned, Matt had the breakfast dishes cleaned and put away and was getting dressed for work. Theresa would get herself ready and walk out the door with him. Thoughts of them being seen together faded, although they both knew it could still be a problem if they were discovered in the right circumstances. When Matt left on his final deployment, she still couldn't see him off at the dock. She and Sophie waited in her car at the end of the point and watched the Derecho sail by. Matt came out on deck and waved to them until he was out of sight. *Just a little longer, and it won't matter anymore.*

Theresa drove Sophie to school that morning, then went to work herself.

Ok, I admit I'm becoming domesticated, but I'll be damned if I grow a big butt and work in the garden until he comes home.

Theresa laughed, reflecting on how much she enjoyed her new life. *I can have both, family and the Navy.*

***

"Hi, Meghan!" Theresa said as she walked towards her office. She was already missing Matt, and it had only been a few hours.

"Good Morning, Commander. There is something on your desk for you," Meghan, the admiral's secretary, replied.

"OK, thanks." Theresa stopped to make herself a coffee before the day started.

Coffee should be one of the main food groups.

She was taking her first sip when she walked into her office, flinging her cap onto a chair. On top of her desk was a single red rose and a lavender colored envelope. A smile grew on her face as she picked up the rose, smelling its fragrance. When she opened the card, she discovered it was from Matt.

Dearest Theresa,

I'm sorry I have to leave you today. Keep your eyes on the horizon, and someday soon, I'll be sailing home to you. Only another couple of months, and we will be together forever. I can't wait.

All my love always,

Matt.

Admiral Kincaid looked into Theresa's office as he walked by. He stopped when he saw her smile, the flower, and the card she was reading.

"From an ardent admirer, no doubt, Commander, "he said.

Theresa looked up, the smile still on her face. "You might say that, Admiral."

"I'm happy for you. You deserve a life outside the Navy." The admiral smiled, then left Theresa to admire her gift.

Maybe not outside the Navy, but the next best thing.

CHAPTER 7

"Ask Commander Leslie to come in, please."

"Yes, sir," Meghan replied. She was giddy, aching to tell someone the secret. Being the Admiral's secretary has its advantages.

She walked down to Commander Leslie's office, leaned in the door, and tried to get her attention. It had been two weeks since Matt gave her the rose and card. The rose had wilted away, but the card was still there to remind her of him every day.

Theresa was looking out the window at the boats and ships going by as she talked with Matt on the phone. He was somewhere on the Atlantic coast on a training mission.

"I miss you too, Matt. I was thinking maybe you and Sophie could move in with me when you get back. It would save us money, and she'd have a yard to play in."

That's when she realized Meghan was waving at her from the hallway.

"Gotta go. Talk to you later. Love You." Theresa hung up and looked at Meghan questioningly.

"The admiral wants you."

"Thanks, Meghan. Why are you so happy?"

Meghan waved for her to hurry. "You'll see!" Meghan opened the door as they reached the Admiral's office, but didn't go in, closing it behind Theresa.

"Sit down, Commander, please." Admiral Kincaid had long ago made it clear he didn't want a lot of formality every time the regular staff passed each other in the course of work, so Theresa sat in a leatherbound chair in front of his desk and waited.

"I got some good news for you," he said, passing a sheaf of paper to her. "The destroyer Phelps has completed refitting and is ready to go to sea for a shakedown prior to joining the Mediterranean fleet. It's a three-year-old Arleigh Burke class destroyer. All the new bells and whistles. You are its brand-new executive officer."

Theresa was thunderstruck at first, but then a broad smile spread across her face.

I can't believe it. Back to sea! No more blue dress Navy!

"There's more. The current captain has six months left before reassignment. If all goes well, six months from now, you will be the new skipper of the Phelps."

Theresa was speechless. *Back to sea AND my own ship in six months! This is unbelievable.*

"The current XO is due to rotate out for a shore assignment six weeks from now. That's when you take over his position. Is that convenient, Theresa?" He was glad for her. He could tell she wasn't happy ashore, and this assignment had been a gift from the Secretary of the Navy, specifically for her.

She didn't even realize he'd called her by her first name. He never got that familiar with his subordinates, except Meghan, of course.

"Absolutely! Yes, sir! Thank you, sir!" *I'm glad I don't faint easily.*

"Meghan, is Lieutenant Ritter there yet?" the Admiral said.

His phone buzzed immediately. "Ok, send her in."

Theresa looked at the admiral quizzically.

"She thinks I don't know," he explained, "but every time she doesn't end the intercom connection, the light on my console still blinks. It's out now. Don't tell her I know."

"Yes, sir!" Theresa managed to say without laughing outright. This much good news was starting to make her giddy. The door opened again, and Theresa's friend Margot came in.

"Reporting, sir."

"Sit down, lieutenant. Read this." He handed her a packet of papers, similar to the one he had given Theresa.

Theresa watched as Margot read the order, her eyes getting bigger the further down the page she went.

"You are a qualified signals officer, I believe, lieutenant," the admiral asked.

Margot could barely contain herself. "Yeah! I mean, uh, yes, sir."

"Ordinarily, I'd give you more than a couple of weeks to get your affairs straight, but the Phelps sails in six weeks, and I want to give you time to refresh your memory before it sails. Any problems with that, Lieutenant?"

"NO! I'll take it! I mean, that's fine, sir," Margot stammered, holding on to Theresa's chair for support.

"That will give your replacements time to get up to speed, too. Train them well. That's all. Congratulations to both of you." Admiral Kincaid stood up and shook their hands across his desk, afraid Lt. Ritter would hug him to death if he got any closer to her.

They walked back to Theresa's office in as dignified a manner as they could. Meghan saw Margot grasp Theresa's hand, squeezing it hard and shaking it (Officers didn't fist-bump, except on rare occasions). Once Theresa's office door closed, though, the squeals of happiness could be heard all over the area.

Wait until she reads that letter, Meghan thought, a smile on her lips too.

When the excitement died down a little, Theresa saw the letter sitting on her desk. It hadn't been there when she left. It was embossed with the US Congress's seal and gold gilded around the edges. Envelopes usually reserved for very special communications.

Although it was labeled "From the office of Congressman Joseph Nichols" on the outside, it contained a letter from Mrs. Nichols.

Dear Commander Leslie,

I hope that this is sufficient recompense for the dishonorable deed my husband inflicted on you. Thanks to you, I was able to make my husband squirm for almost the whole election cycle until he finally agreed to my terms. I will keep a tight leash on him from now on, but keep that card I gave you handy in case he backslides.

Best Regards,

Rachel Nichols

"Holy Shit! We are out of purgatory and back in the Blue Water Navy because she wanted to teach him a lesson? That is one tough bitch!" Margot exclaimed.

***

Theresa was bursting with happiness. She was so used to shore duty that it hadn't occurred to her how this affected her plans with Matt. She was sitting in her car on the parking lot, cell phone out, about to call him when it hit her.

Six weeks? Matt will be back from deployment and ready to start his new job. It'll be months before we return. Our wedding plans are destroyed.

She put her cell phone away and just sat there, a look of concern on her face.

He sacrificed so much! How can I do this to him?

***

It was the weekend. Theresa had Sophie and her sister's daughter, Julie, over for a sleepover. It had been nonstop madness and mayhem since they'd arrived at her house. They'd eaten lunch, and Sophie went down for a nap. Julie, a year older, was asleep on the couch. They'd spent the morning playing dress up, modeling some of Theresa's clothes and uniforms in front of the mirror. Lipstick, various powders, and eyeliners were strewn everywhere. Theresa had videoed some of it and sent it to Matt. She was sitting in the kitchen, appreciating the quiet and the cup of coffee she had, when her computer beeped. Matt was calling.

"Hi, Matt," Theresa said. She wouldn't dare call him anything else because if he weren't using headphones, everyone on the PC would know in less than an hour.

"Hey, Therese," Matt said. "I loved that video. Can I talk to Sophie?"

"Sorry, Matt. She is napping. What's new?" Theresa asked as she sipped her coffee. Matt said, "Our tour has been extended so we can do dog and pony shows for Canadian brass. They are considering buying a few of the new PCs when they come out, and want to see what this old one can do first. We will be on our way home two weeks after the last display."

Matt's camera view bounced a lot, making it difficult for the autofocus camera on top of his computer to keep focus.

"Looks rough there," Theresa commented, refilling her cup.

"We are in port, but a gale is brewing up. Batten down the hatches time," he replied.

"Matt, I have something to tell you," Theresa said, sitting her mug on the table.

Matt smiled before he replied, "You're pregnant, and I'm going to be a father soon."

Theresa shifted uncomfortably." Nooo. I've received orders. I'll probably be gone when you get home."

Matt's smile faded. It was quiet for a while." Where to?"

"I'm going to a destroyer, the Phelps. I'll be the XO." She could tell Matt wasn't happy with this news. She hated breaking the news like this, but if his tour was extended, she would be at sea when he returned home.

She could see Matt's mind shifting, and the smile returned to his face. "That's great, Theresa. I'm happy for you."

"I'm sorry, Matt. I had no idea this was coming. I've told your mom and dad, but I was waiting for you to get back before I told Sophie."

"I understand. Hey, look, I've got to go. I'll talk to you tomorrow. Bye."

"Matt!" Theresa said, but he had already cut the feed.

Oh, my God. I've hurt him. A transfer was always possible, but we never considered what would happen if it occurred.

***

"Commander Leslie! Welcome aboard." Theresa saluted and then handed her orders to Captain Nixon.

"I understand you have had an interesting career so far," he said, tossing her orders on his desk.

"Yes, sir. This is my second destroyer. I was on a fleet auxiliary and, of course, the Derecho."

"In command of the Derecho, in fact," he remarked.

"Yes, sir."

Captain Nixon leaned on his desk and folded his arms. He had a stern look on his face.

"Well, Commander, I'd like to make something clear before you get started. You are with the big boys now. I expect things to be taut and by regulations. I don't know how you ran your little PC, but on this destroyer, uniforms will be squared away at all times. Your shoes will be shined. Regulation haircut. I hold Captain's Mast twice a month and deal swiftly with any breaches of discipline or inefficiency, got it?"

"Yes, sir," Theresa said.

She noted that, unlike most ship captains she had worked for, he hadn't told her "At Ease." *Boot camp BS all over again.*

"In addition to your regular duties and watches, you will inspect this ship from one end to the other, top to bottom, and bring me a report on any deficiencies you find every week. There are always deficiencies, Commander—one last thing. When we leave port, you will collect all cellphones, laptops, or any other communication devices the crew has, including your own. They will be locked away. The ship's computers will not be used for anything but official duties. You will talk to the lieutenant in charge of the computers and bring me a printout of any unauthorized requests or transmissions. We will be on communications blackout until otherwise notified. Got it?"

"Yes, sir," Theresa said, *Captain Queeg. *

Captain Nixon replied, "Very well, that's all." He turned his back and started leafing through Theresa's file.

***

Theresa was on the bridge as the Phelps left port. Though a civilian pilot was on board to navigate the ship through shallow waters and shoals, Captain Nixon trusted no one and watched him like a hawk. There was no unofficial talk or noise of any kind on the bridge that you would find on any other destroyer. Deathly quiet.

I bet the last XO was happy when that school came up for him.

 Theresa could see Admiral Kincaid's offices from her station as they sailed by. She knew roughly where Matt's apartment and her house were.

It was hard enough to say goodbye to Sophie.

I haven't heard a word from Matt since I told him about my new assignment. Why won't he talk to me? We have to work this out. With this communication blackout, I may not hear from him for a long time now. It's going to be a hard six months.

On the second day, when the Phelps was well out to sea, Captain Nixon assembled his senior staff in the wardroom. Theresa noticed that none of the old crew sat down before the captain arrived and took his seat at the head of the table.

"Sit," he said. When everyone was seated, he tossed a manila envelope on the table and leaned forward.

"Before we left port, I received new orders from Admiral Kincaid. We are no longer going to the Mediterranean. We are going to the Red Sea to support operations against Houthi rebel drones, missiles, and suicide boats. I assume everyone knows what I'm talking about, but just in case you haven't been paying attention, Houthi rebels have been fighting the legitimate government in Yemen for years. So long as they left everyone else alone, we left them alone. Recently, they have intercepted or fired on legitimate shipping in the Red Sea and the Gulf of Aden. They claim they only attack ships owned by or enroute to Israel, but that's bullshit. In response, the world's navies are escorting merchant ships that want to use that passage to the Suez Canal instead of going the long way around the Horn of Africa. Our role is purely defensive, but if tasked, we will attack ground targets in Yemen. Since we have just received a slew of upgrades, we will run system checks and drills until I feel we are ready. No live ordinance is to be expended. XO, launch drones day and night at odd hours and have crews go to general quarters and track them. I will accept nothing less than perfection, got it?"

Theresa replied, "Yes, sir."

"With one notable exception," Nixon stared at Theresa," no one here has ever been under fire. I can't help that. Do your jobs. Any questions?"

"XO, when will we arrive at our station?"

Theresa did a quick estimation in her head." At this speed, four to five days."

"I didn't ask for a maybe. When will we arrive there?" he said acidly.

"I'll get with the navigator and get you the correct information after we adjourn, sir."

 Christ, you just told me we were going there! How the hell do I know when we'll arrive?

Nixon shoved the envelope in front of her. "Fifteen minutes, Commander. The references are in there."

"Yes, sir."

"Dismissed." Everyone shot to their feet as the captain stood up, glared around the room, and left.

***

"General Quarters! General Quarters, man your battle stations!"

Theresa shot up from her bunk, looking at her clock. *0300! What the hell is he trying to prove?*

Every night, sometime in the late watch, Nixon would have a General Quarters drill. This was in addition to those Theresa was required to do during more normal hours. It was wrecking the crew's sleep and keeping them on edge. Crewmen had started wearing their clothes to bed to save time. No one wanted to be the last weapon or system to signal their readiness and receive a blistering rebuke from the Captain. It was definitely affecting crew morale. Grumbling, a sailor's tradition even on good days, was increasingly directed at Nixon.

She met Captain Nixon in the CIC (Combat Information Center) in moments. The integrated displays of all US combat ships' surveillance systems gave each commanding officer a detailed picture of vessels and air traffic in the area on an almost instantaneous plotting board that hung in the CIC. The days of the captain standing on the bridge with a spyglass, trying to observe only what he could see close by, were long gone. Most of that work was now concentrated in the Combat Information Center behind the bridge. The move or click of a mouse gave instant information on any boat, ship, or aircraft well over the horizon. This revolutionary system came with its own problems—too much information. Multiple operators in the CIC shared their screen information with the master plot, with symbols and colors to indicate the vessels. That helped a lot, but it had its own limitations. Too many boats and small craft that worked in the area did not have IFF (Identification Friend or Foe electronic signals) and were too small to be seen easily by radar. The old Mark One eyeball still had a place.

"Commander, Launch drone!"

"Yes, sir." Theresa picked up a sound phone and called the drone shack in the ship's rear. In a moment, someone picked up the phone. "Launch a drone."

"Yes, Ma'am, on the way." The voice disconnected. The radar operators quickly picked up the launch, tracking it astern and around the ship.

"Are weapons manned and ready, XO?" Nixon demanded. Theresa looked at the weapons officer. All but one crew were manned and locked on the target.

"All but one, sir." She replied," The last green light lit almost as she said it. "Last one online and ready, sir."

"Who was last, XO?" Nixon demanded, clicking an old-fashioned stopwatch.

Theresa picked up the sound phone and called the last crew to come online.

In a moment, she hung up and turned to the captain.

"HELIOS (High Energy Laser with Integrated Optical-dazzler and Surveillance), sir. The laser array showed a fault on the computer screen. It took them some time to reset it."

"I didn't ask for an excuse, XO! I want a full report in the morning and your recommendations for disciplinary actions!"

"Sir," Theresa protested. "They were less than a minute behind everyone else."

Captain Nixon strode over to Theresa, yelling in her face," I will not have them or any other member of the ship's company turn in a substandard performance!"

Everyone in CIC was studiously avoiding looking at Nixon screaming at Theresa.

Nixon looked Theresa up and down, then continued his rant," That includes you, XO! I told you when you came aboard, you were to be dressed appropriately according to regulations at all times!" He grabbed the unbuttoned shirt pocket on her uniform, yanking it around and jiggling her breast. "You got away with this on your little patrol craft, COMMANDER, but not here! If I catch you out of uniform again, you can expect a reprimand in your jacket! How will that look on your next evaluation, COMMANDER? Fix it!"

Nixon stared at Theresa, daring her to say anything. She buttoned the pocket and returned to attention.

"You're not going to cry, are you, Miss Leslie?" He spoke just loud enough for everyone to hear.

"You must be joking, Captain," she replied loudly. "It will take more than you to make me cry, SIR!"

"We'll see," Nixon said softly.

***

Theresa looked up from her paperwork when she heard a knock on her cabin door.

"Come in!" She yelled. When no one opened the door, she went to see who was there.

"Hey, Theresa, I thought you could use a break." It was her friend, Margot, carrying two mugs of coffee.

"Hi, Margot. Come on in." She took one of the mugs from Margot and pulled up a second chair.

"I hear the captain really reamed you out last night," Margot said, leaning back on her chair.

"In front of the crew, no less," Theresa replied, blowing on her coffee.

"An unbuttoned pocket? A crew slower than the rest because of a fault in a system? That's rather petty. Any creamer in here? I forgot to bring some."

Theresa opened a drawer in her desk and tossed Margot two packets.

"I'm not sure what he is trying to prove, keeping his crew on edge all the time. We arrive in the Red Sea tomorrow. He's already worn out half the crew with these constant drills. Even if they sleep at their battle stations, they can't get ready much faster."

"How are you holding up?" Margot asked.

"This unnecessary com's blackout makes me miss..." Theresa caught herself.

"Margot, can you keep a secret?"

"If it's a good one," she replied," Give."

"I'm engaged."

Margot looked at her and then smiled broadly. She could barely contain herself from jumping out of her chair.

"Who? Tell me, tell me!"

"I met him a long time ago, before that Mahan incident. You've never met him. His name is Matt. He has a beautiful five-year-old daughter. Six by now. I couldn't even call and wish her happy birthday because of this blackout."

"That's great, Therese! When is the wedding? You'd better invite me, or I'll be pissed at you."

"Actually, I was going to ask you to be my maid of honor."

Margot squealed in delight." Me? You don't want me. I'll get arrested at your bachelorette party for sure."

"Nope, you're it. We haven't set a date yet. This deployment screwed up all of our plans. Matt was upset when I told him, and I haven't been able to talk to him since."

"Maybe I can sneak a message through for you," Margot said.

Theresa set her cup down and leaned in towards Margot. "Absolutely not. For one, it's against orders, and the captain has me reporting any unauthorized transmissions daily. You do anything, and both of us will pay. I'll contact him when we get to a neutral port. Hell, people used to write letters to each other, for crying out loud. By the time we get a ship-to-ship resupply, my letter will be too thick to mail."

Margot checked her watch. "Gotta go, duty calls."

"Margot, I mean it. Don't do anything, please?"

Margot looked at Theresa for a while, shrugged, and nodded. "OK."

Dear Matt,

I'm sorry, I have to use snail mail. We are on comms blackout.

The orders for Margot and I came out of the blue. I should say, Congressman Nichols' wife, Rachel, came out of the blue. An apology for the way her asshole husband acted. Rachel is one formidable woman.

We didn't have much time to talk before I left. I could see the hurt in your eyes the last time we talked. You bent over backwards to make it possible for us to be married. Moving to the Navy Reserve was a difficult decision. Your eyes were set on what's just over the horizon, just like mine. Sailing the world, fighting bad guys, and maybe commanding a ship of your own someday. When these orders came, all our plans were blown away. Please tell me what's on your mind. I miss you.

I'd love to have had all the flowers and music, a wonderful wedding, but it isn't necessary. Bring a chaplain with you to the dock. He can marry us on the ship. If that doesn't work, I'll fly to Vegas or Tijuana if I have to to marry you. I've caught the best fish in the ocean, and I'm not about to let it go. I can't wait to be your wife.

Love,

Theresa.

PS -Fill me in on all the adventures of you, Sophie, and Zelda. I wish I'd been there for Sophie's birthday party.

***

"Be seated," Captain Nixon said, sighing as he flopped into his chair. A map of the area appeared on the large wall monitor on the bulkhead.

"Our assigned area is the main anchorage in the Gulf of Aden. We protect ships in the anchorage and escort them as far as the Seven Brothers Islands near the Bab El Mandeb strait, where we hand off to the destroyer Allen. A few other nations patrol the anchorage also. Only a few minor attempts have been made to attack shipping in the anchorage. The area of significant concern is as we approach Seven Brothers Island. "

Nixon clicked a button, changing the picture.

"This picture lists the significant attacks in the last ninety days. Almost all of them start in or before the Strait. In one case, they actually took over a ship by force; therefore, any helicopter leaving Yemen is now subject to being shot down. They know that, so it's unlikely they'll try that again.

"The Navy strike group has pummeled Houthi missile sites and command centers with limited effect. Therefore, our job is critical."

"Until further notice, we will be on a modified general quarters status. If possible, all weapons systems will be manned and ready, but at reduced manning. I want to be prepared to launch at a moment's notice, 24/7."

Nixon looked at Theresa. "You want to say anything, Commander?"

"Sir?" Theresa asked, baffled at the question.

"You don't think that's overtaxing the crew, do you?"

"No, sir. We have a modified scheme for that kind of operational status."

"It's not going to be for only a few days like your little incident. The big Navy stays engaged for months at a time."

"I realize that, Captain." Theresa was perplexed as to why Nixon was being so snarky.

"I and I alone will authorize firing any weapon. We will not have any accidents or friendly fire incidents. I will be alerted promptly, regardless of the time. Got it, Commander?"

"Yes, sir. 24/7," Theresa responded.

"You don't think that's being petty, Commander?" Nixon's stare became uncomfortable." The captain has ultimate authority on this ship, right, Commander?"

Theresa's eyebrow rose. *Margot and I were talking about him being petty.*

"Unquestionably, sir."

Nixon turned to look at the other officers present. "Any of you have problems with that?"

No one dared say anything, staring at the picture on the computer screen instead. Nixon stood up to leave. The ship's officers rose as one until he left the room.

As Theresa met with the navigator to plot out the routes, tides, and obstructions they may encounter, the officer in charge of the engine room touched her arm.

"XO, do you have a minute?" Lt. Thomas, a short, muscular man with prematurely graying hair, was one of the Phelps crew before the refit. He walked out on deck, and Theresa, mystified, followed. He shut the hatch behind him, offering her a cigarette.

"No thanks," Theresa said.

"The captain won't allow smoking in the wardroom," he explained. They stood behind a bulkhead bulge to block the wind as he lit the cigarette, exhaling gratefully.

"Xo, I don't know why the captain has been so outrageous since we left port. He seems to have a particular dislike for you."

"I can deal with it, Joseph, isn't it?"

"Yes, Ma'am. Joe's fine. Captain Nixon wasn't like that on our last cruise. He wasn't lax or anything, but he was fair. Rumor has it that he has never been in combat. He was in shore installations his entire career until recently. Maybe that's why he is so hard on you."

"I can't help that, Joe," Theresa responded, leaning against the bulkhead.

Joe nodded, taking a deep drag on his cigarette. "A friend of mine in personnel let slip he was overlooked for admiral last time. He's never been to sea before this command. He'll probably retire as a Captain if he is passed over again."

Joe took a last puff on his cigarette before crushing it and field-stripping it, putting the paper in his pocket. "At any rate, Ma'am, I just wanted you to know the officers like you and see what's happening."

"Thanks, that means a lot."

***

"An unidentified aerial object is approaching; it is probably a drone of some type. Five miles at 500 feet, no visual reported," the air radar operator said.

"Weapons track and standby, CAPTAIN TO CIC!" Theresa announced. This was the third time the captain had been called in the last 24 hours. Twice, the aerial object had turned out to be large flocks of birds flying over the anchorage. This did not improve his mood. Captain Nixon had ordered double lookouts to verify what the computer told them.

Captain Nixon appeared a moment later. "CAPTAIN ON DECK, "a sailor announced.

"What is it this time? Another flock of birds, XO?"

Theresa replied." I'll go look myself, sir."

 She walked quickly to the bridge and grabbed a pair of binoculars. At first, there appeared to be nothing to see, but then she saw a small object flying swiftly at low altitude heading towards a merchantman. Theresa grabbed the sound phone to the CIC, "Confirmed, drone inbound one mile skimming the deck."

"Yes, Ma'am, drone inbound one mile, skimming the deck," the sailor repeated.

In the CIC, the sailor yelled, "Confirmed inbound drone captain."

"Is she sure this time? Ask port lookouts to verify," Captain Nixon retorted.

Theresa watched as the drone gained altitude before plunging to the deck of the merchantman behind them.

The drone impacted just aft of the merchant's bridge structure, followed by a large flame. Theresa watched helplessly as the ship began burning.

"Tell the Captain the drone impacted; the ship is aflame," Theresa advised over the phone.

***

Anyone passing by Captain Nixon's cabin could hear the yelling going on inside, even with the door closed.

"Your dereliction of duty caused the merchant ship we were escorting to be damaged! It's fortunate for you it didn't sink, or I'd confine you to quarters pending court-martial." Nixon's face was deep red, his voice shrill.

"We followed your written standing orders, Captain," Theresa said as calmly as possible. "Any court-martial board could read the ship's S.O.s and see that, sir."

Nixon was now nose to nose with Theresa, jabbing his finger at her face.

"Don't try to play sea lawyer with me, Commander! You let an enemy drone close within five miles of this ship and did nothing to destroy it! Nothing! Your lack of initiative could have killed people over there. All you managed to do is embarrass this ship!"

"Sir, you were notified while the drone was five miles from the target. Weapons were tracking it. Your specific orders, in front of every officer on this ship, expressly forbade anyone to fire on a target except you, sir!"

"You are trying to blame me? You were the officer on duty! You are responsible!"

"Sir, you require visual verification of the target. The drone was only a mile away when I saw it and relayed it to CIC. There was still time to engage it. I do not know why that didn't occur. I watched it impact the merchantman. I will investigate, get statements from all crewmembers involved, and have it on your desk tomorrow!"

"You will do nothing of the kind, Commander! You are confined to quarters until otherwise notified, got it? Your cabin! Nowhere else!"

"Yes, sir! Is that all, sir?" Theresa said, her temper barely in check.

"Get the hell out of my face!" Nixon yelled, spittle flying from his mouth.

***

Theresa lay on her bunk, staring at the overhead pipes. She'd written a couple of letters to Matt. A third one lay in its envelope, waiting for her to finish it.

I don't ever remember being homesick until I got on this ship. I could always text or talk to Mom and Dad, Jackie, Matt, or anyone I wanted to. With this blackout in effect,

I have no idea what's going on. What's Matt feeling? Has Sophie been doing good in school? There's no way to know. I've never felt this isolated. I can't even get off the ship when we dock tomorrow—punishment for making Nixon look bad.

One good thing, at least. Slowing down and writing a letter makes me realize how important family is to me.

***

A knock on the door stirred Theresa from her dark mood. "Hey, jailbird, open up, it's dinnertime!"

Margot. It would be her. A smile grew on Theresa's face just thinking of her stalwart friend.

"Doors open; come on in."

Margot opened the door with one hand, precariously balancing a tray in the other. "You know, if I have to act like your waitress, at least you could get off your ass and open the door."

Theresa burst out laughing at her over-the-top friend.

"As I recall, you did that professionally for a while," Theresa said.

"It was in high school, for spending money," Margot shot back.

"Too bad. I'm a lousy tipper anyway," Theresa said, taking the cover off the tray.

"So, how are you holding up?" Margot asked, pouring something into small plastic cups for both of them and handing one to her. Theresa looked at her questioningly, but drank it down when Margot did. Whatever it was, it hit Theresa hard. "What the hell was that!" she said, coughing.

"Water," Margot said, her face modeling perfect innocence.

Theresa's eyebrows shot up. "The hell it was!" she gasped.

Margot shrugged, tucking the flask under Theresa's mattress, "Ok, Irish water, distilled."

"Is there any rule you won't break?" Theresa said, finally catching her breath.

"Don't know, haven't found one yet. You want me to mail those?" indicating the letters on Theresa's desk.

"If you would, thanks. I can't leave the ship either."

Margot grabbed the envelopes, stuffing them inside her blouse.

"If you see anything a six-year-old girl would love, could you buy it for me? I want to send her something for her birthday." Theresa handed her a wad of money.

"Damn, what do you want, a real flying carpet or something? I don't need all of that."

"If you see something small for Matt, too, if you don't mind, anything left over will pay your bar bill."

"Hell, you didn't give me that much! I'll see what I can do. I have to get something for my husband anyway."

"Thanks, Margot. You are a dear friend." Theresa hugged her, holding her tight for a moment.

"Don't get all sentimental and squishy on me!" Margot said, returning the hug.

When she got back to her bunk, Margot counted the money Theresa gave her.

Shit. I'm going to have to hire someone to carry me back to the ship if I drink this much!

Inside the mass of bills was a business card. Margot remembered Rachel Nichols giving Theresa that card in case her husband tried to get even. She thought about it for a moment before placing the card in Theresa's unsealed letter, along with a note.

Two days later, when they were back on station in the Gulf of Aden, Theresa was released from her confinement without an explanation and resumed her regular duties. She reviewed the ship's standing orders, realizing something had changed. The XO or the officer of the day now had the authority to fire at any imminent threat at their discretion. "All standard protocols apply. Any IFF (Identification Friend or Foe) not matching aircraft or boats known to be in the vicinity, or aircraft not displaying IFF, may be fired upon if radio challenges on International Guard frequencies are not immediately replied to. The captain will still be notified of any unknown contacts immediately."

It was a tacit acknowledgment from Nixon that he had been wrong.

***

Inspection? He wants a full-blown junk on the bunk inspection in a war zone?

Captain Nixon had announced a snap inspection of all crew berthing areas. Everything ironed, shined, and polished, laid out on your rack in the approved manner. He started with Theresa's cabin.

Nixon walked in, scrutinizing everything. He even looked in the trash can, sniffing old paper cups.

What is he looking for? A gnawing suspicion grew in Theresa's mind. *The whiskey? How would he know about that?*

Nixon became frustrated, telling the young officer following him with a clipboard, "General cleanliness, unsatisfactory. These shoes," he stepped on the shoes, grinding a scuff in the polish," are unsatisfactory also."

Nixon stepped in front of Theresa, offensively close. "Your quarters are sloppy, Commander. Fix it. Your punishment is to continue the inspection in all berthing areas of this ship. Lt. Morgan," he indicated the officer with the clipboard, "will write down all discrepancies you find and anything you might 'overlook.' He will give me a report this afternoon. Understood, XO?"

"Yes, sir," Theresa replied. *Your lackey is here to watch me.*

"When you are finished, return to your quarters and scrub it until I say it's clean. That's all."

Theresa returned to her quarters late that day, having inspected every sailor not on duty's gear and their living spaces. As much as she wanted to, she could not sleep.

What did I do to deserve this? Gigging sailors if their bunk display wasn't perfect, if their underwear wasn't perfectly aligned with the diagram in the SOP's? This bullshit is for peacetime, not now when people are shooting at us. Nixon should know he's destroying crew morale. He doesn't seem to care. Hold on. Put up with this bullshit. Two more months, that's what Admiral Kincaid said. Two more months...

CHAPTER 8

Two weeks later, Theresa was in CIC monitoring the air and seas around the anchorage. Captain Nixon had been called to a conference with the Task Force commander, leaving her in charge. "Sir," A young lieutenant, the current officer of the day, said. "Lookouts advise a small boat has left shore and is heading for us at high speed. It is not displaying any flags or squawking a GPS tag."

"Distance?"

"Two miles and closing. It's on an intercept course with the tanker we are escorting."

"Put us between them and the tanker. Alert the gun crews. Broadcast warning messages." (Loudspeakers that play messages in various Arabic dialects warn the boat not to come close, or it will be fired upon. Radio transmissions in the local dialects are also broadcast.)

" Warn them away as soon as they are in range."

"Aye, aye, sir," the nervous lieutenant said.

Theresa studied the main screen for a moment before grabbing a pair of binoculars and walking out to the bridge. She could see the low boat and the rooster tail wake it created as it closed with them.

Standard suicide boat profile. I'm not letting that thing anywhere near us.

"Fire a warning shot in front of them, Main gun mount," Theresa yelled over the loudspeaker noise. "HELIOS target and engage, optical dazzler."

(Laser used to burn out drones' sensors and blind/destroy them)

"Yes, sir," the lieutenant said. The forward gun mount fired a moment later, its boom resonating throughout the ship. Within seconds, the round exploded close in front of the speeding boat. Whoever was at the controls faltered, veering away at first, then continued to close on the tanker.

"OD, sink that bastard!" Theresa yelled loudly.

"Yes, sir!"

In moments, machine gun and cannon fire converged on the speeding boat. Rounds were chewing up the hull before any evasive action could be attempted. The craft lost way immediately, wallowing in its wake, followed by the detonation of its explosive-packed hull. A massive cloud of smoke and fire shot up, mixing with bits of debris flying over the doomed boat. The noise and shockwave carried to the bridge of the Phelps.

"Holy hell!" the OD said, ducking instinctively.

"Lieutenant, cease-fire. Notify the squadron commander that we've destroyed a suicide boat and give them our location. What was the distance at its closest point of approach?"

The lieutenant picked up the phone and contacted CIC. "Half a mile, sir!"

"Very well. Tell them that, too. Before you do, come over here." Theresa waved him over.

"Sir?" The lieutenant said, standing in front of her.

"Lieutenant, how good is your eyesight?" Theresa asked.

"Twenty-twenty, sir!" he replied. They stood there in silence until the lieutenant realized her meaning. An embarrassed smile crossed his face." Excuse me- Ma'am!"

"Thank you. For a moment, I thought you were blind. That's all, lieutenant."

After he left, Theresa had to laugh. *Poor kid. That was probably the first time he's ever seen a shot fired in anger.*

***

"Theresa! Theresa!" When she looked to see who was calling her, she saw Margot at the entrance to the bridge, waving at her.

She's going to pee herself if she doesn't calm down.

"Shhhh, come over here," Theresa said. "The captain demands a quiet bridge."

Margot walked over, handing Theresa a message. "I had to deliver this myself."

Theresa read the message, then, disbelieving, reread it. "This can't be right. He had another two months."

"I asked for a repeat," Margot said." Captain Nixon has been relieved. He's on his way stateside."

"What the hell happened?" Theresa asked.

 Margot shrugged," Don't know, don't care. Finish reading the message, Captain."

Now, Theresa was really confused. She reread the message again, including something she hadn't read before. She looked at Margot in amazement. "I'm the new captain of the Phelps!"

"Yep, your new XO is being flown out here tomorrow."

"Holy shit. OK, here's my first order as C.O. The message blackout is lifted. All personnel who had their phones and laptops confiscated will see you to get them back. Instruct them in message security as you hand out the devices. In the meantime, set up a link through the ship's computer and let people call home immediately."

***

"Attention!" The officers in the wardroom snapped to attention as Theresa entered. From the smiles on their faces, she knew she wasn't going to tell them anything they didn't already know.

"At Ease. Everyone, sit and relax." They waited until Theresa took her seat and then sat down.

"Apparently, the word has gotten around the ship already, but for the record, I am your new captain. Captain Nixon has been sent home for unspecified reasons. Effective immediately, the following changes apply. Number one, except for formal occasions or if dignitaries are present, this bullshit boot camp stuff will cease immediately. The next person I see snapping to attention when I enter the room or waiting for me to sit down first will be sorry.

"Second, and this is already in effect. All laptops, cellphones, and tablets will be returned, subject to instruction on communications security for all personnel.

"Third, uniform regulations will remain in force, but don't be assholes about it. I expect shiny shoes and squared-away uniforms at inspections and when liberty is granted before the crew leaves the ship. At all other times, if someone has an unbuttoned button, tell them to button it and move on. If something in the engine room or any other space requires uniform modifications to keep a reasonable level of comfort, act on your own initiative. If the new XO or I have a problem with it, we'll let you know.

"Fourth and finally, I will not tolerate any officer or NCO bullying or berating anyone at any time. You can discipline someone quietly and respectfully. If someone needs discipline beyond your informal reprimands or if the situation demands it, I will convene a captain's mast. Otherwise, handle it yourself."

Theresa slumped back in her chair. "Keep your crew and equipment up to the mark but treat them like humans. If you can think of anything I've missed, let me know. I'm sure as time goes by, we will have some adjustments to make. I will not lead this ship based on fear. Any questions?"

Theresa opened the folder in front of her and passed a stack of papers around. "Take one. It's a copy of what I've just covered. We have a good crew and a good ship. You be the good leaders. That's all, dismissed."

Theresa looked, expecting to see people heading for the exits, but no one moved from their seats. They all sat there quietly, not talking.

"Does someone want me to reread rule number one?" The officers broke into laughter and stood up, stretching and talking amongst themselves. The relief was palpable in the room.

***

Theresa helped the sailors stow away Captain Nixon's personal effects. Confidential orders and other papers in the cabin needed to be safeguarded. She wasn't concerned that the CPO and his assistant would steal anything or damage it on purpose, though the crew universally disliked Captain Nixon; she knew these sailors were trustworthy. It was just that the sooner she moved her stuff, the sooner the new XO could bring his own gear in. Among the usual items: uniforms, trophies and awards, family pictures, etc. Theresa found a CD marked "Leslie" and a letter from Matt to her dated over a week ago.

What the hell, my own CD? That bastard was holding my mail, too!

She took the CD to her cabin, inserted it into the drive, and sat back to view it.

Instead of the video she expected, her and Margot's voices came through.

"Come in!"

"Hey, Theresa, I thought you could use a break."

"Hi, Margot. Come on in."

"I hear the captain really reamed you out last night."

"In front of the crew, no less."

"An unbuttoned pocket? A crew slower than the rest because of a fault in a system? That's rather petty. Any creamer in here? I forgot to bring some."

Theresa sat back in disbelief. *He bugged my room? Why? None of this makes sense.*

Theresa began searching her cabin. It didn't take long to discover a small voice-activated device on one of the shelves near her desk.

How long has he been listening in? Not too long, I guess. It explains some of his comments and the 'snap' inspection, but doesn't answer the big question: Why?

Theresa sat on her bunk and opened the letter. She was hungry for any news from the real world. It felt like ages.

Dearest Theresa,

Sophie and I read your letters over and over again. It was so good to hear from you. I've never heard of a communications blackout this extensive on any ship.

I admit I was disappointed when you told me you were shipping out. I was looking forward to our wedding, and I guess I took it too hard. If I'd known about this blackout, which no one else over there is doing, by the way, I wouldn't have been so childish.

You and I are meant for each other, Therese. If I have to wait a little longer, I will.

Sophie's doing fine. Her music teacher is having all the students buy plastic flutes so they can learn to play. There will be no more peaceful evenings at home for a while. She sends her love and this picture. I think it's a ship.

Hurry home, honey. We all miss you.

Love,

Matt.

Theresa unfolded the picture. Despite the waves and sail, you'd have a hard time convincing anyone it was actually a ship. Either birds or airplanes were flying overhead. Theresa loved it, taping it to her bulkhead wall as soon as she got resettled. The relief Theresa felt hearing that everything was ok at home made a world of difference. She realized that tears were running down her cheeks, but she didn't care. Theresa clutched the letter and picture tightly, thanking God that everything was fine at home.

***

Theresa was so happy to talk to Matt again that she didn't yell at Margot for returning her laptop before the crew got theirs.

"Matt! I'm so happy to see you!" She was sitting in her new quarters. She'd authorized personnel who could be spared to get their electronics and relief for those on duty, so everyone could get their stuff as soon as possible. That helped Margot, too; she didn't have to stop what she was doing and help one or two crewmen in drips and drabs all day. Anyone who could was calling home, talking to their loved ones, or in some cases, their bookies.

"Theresa! What happened? I was worried sick."

"It's a long story, Matt. The captain confiscated all electronics for 'security reasons.' Anyone caught using the ship's computers to call home was disciplined. I wasn't even allowed off the ship, can you believe that? I wrote you some letters, and Margot mailed them for me."

"Yeah, about that..." Matt began. Before he could finish, Sophie climbed onto his lap and sat down. "Hi, Miss Theresa!"

Theresa was almost overcome with happiness." Hi Sophie! What have you been doing?"

For the next ten minutes, Sophie related virtually everything that had happened since Theresa left.

"You loved that doll Miss Theresa sent you, right?" Matt prompted.

Sophie nodded with enthusiasm and flew to her room to get it.

"Theresa, before she gets back..."

"General Quarters, inbound missile! Captain to the bridge!" Blared over the PA system. Bells and klaxon horns followed a second later.

"Matt, I have to go! I love you!" Theresa said before hurriedly signing off and sprinting to the CIC.

"CAPTAIN ON DECK! Someone yelled as she entered the room.

"Report!"

"High-speed missile inbound, ten miles. Launched from land. All crews report ready and tracking."

Shit! It will be here before we can...

"Launch countermeasures! Twenty degrees left rudder, flank speed. HELIO and Phalanx are weapons free to engage!" Theresa shouted.

Theresa barely made it to the bridge in time to witness the engagement. She heard the ripping sound of the Phalanx Close-In Weapons System (CIWS). (The Phalanx is a last ditch defense weapon against incoming threats at short range. It can fire 4,500 20 mm armor-piercing tungsten core or depleted uranium rounds a minute.) The blur of the missile erupted into a fireball as the stream of rounds swept through it. In an instant, the missile plunged into the sea. It had been so close that debris from the explosion pelted the ship, some striking the bridge and shattering a window. Those on bridge watch were knocked down by the concussion of the blast but otherwise unhurt.

"OD, any other threats on the radar?"

"No, Ma'am, no threats," he replied, his voice shaking.

"Check all sections; advise if we have any injuries or damage." Theresa flopped into her captain's chair while the lieutenant checked. Her head was pounding, and she was gasping for breath. Her fists were clenched to keep her hands from shaking.

That thing was coming right at me! Just like the Mahan.

Theresa forced herself to appear as calm as possible by the time the officer of the day returned.

"A few cuts and bruises, Ma'am. Minor damage where debris struck the ship. Some paint will take care of most of it."

Theresa knew everyone was watching to see if she would tear into the young lieutenant like their former captain had.

If I do, all the goodwill I have garnered will blow away like smoke.

Theresa stood up slowly, appearing to tower over the shorter lieutenant. She motioned for him to follow her out onto the bridge wing, closing the hatch behind them. Theresa leaned back against the bridge window and put her foot on the lowest railing. The lieutenant stood at stiff attention, his face red, anxiously waiting for the rebuke he knew was coming.

"At ease, lieutenant, relax. Tell me what happened."

"Ma'am, the radar picked up the launch a few minutes before I called you. I waited until I confirmed it was heading for us. I put the weapons crews on alert just in case.

"I'm sorry, Captain. I didn't realize how fast those things move."

"I see." Theresa noticed that the lieutenant had a pack of cigarettes protruding from his pocket.

"Lieutenant, if it will help you calm your nerves, you can light one up. I don't mind."

"Thank you, Ma'am." He pulled the pack from his pocket and lit one, accidentally blowing smoke across Theresa's face.

"Downwind, if you please," she said, waving the smoke away.

"Sorry, Ma'am."

Theresa sighed. *Nixon has all of them scared shitless. He's unsure what to do.*

"In future, if you see anything, a missile launch, a drone, a boat, anything that could be a threat to this ship or any ship, don't wait. "

"Ma'am, Captain Nixon..." he began.

"Is gone," Theresa said firmly, brushing her hair out of her face. She suddenly realized she had left her cabin without her hat, and her hair was blowing in the wind.

I must look like I'm on a pleasure cruise.

"If you make a mistake, a general quarters that proves to be unnecessary, so be it. I won't hold it against you. It's better than being blown out of the water, ok?"

"Yes, Ma'am."

"OK. Go send a report to the squadron commander and resume your duties."

"Thanks, Ma'am." The lieutenant said, a lopsided grin on his face. "I'll do better."

Theresa went across the bridge, heading to her cabin. "OD has the conn," she announced loudly. The rest of the bridge crew seemed confused. They had expected at least a dressing down for the officer of the day, but from their angle through the window glass, it looked more like a casual talk. They didn't know what to make of it. Meanwhile, out of sight, the young officer of the day vomited over the railing.

***

Incoming missile, five miles and closing. Captain, what do we do? Do something, captain! It's going to hit us! Oh, My God!

Theresa sat up in her bunk, screaming and thrashing around. She fumbled for the light switch, then sat there gasping for breath. *I couldn't move. I just sat there and let it kill us all. Why couldn't I move? Do something?*

Theresa shook her head, trying to shake off the nightmare.

It was just a dream! Just a dream! Calm down.

She sat there holding her head before finally getting up and getting dressed. *There's no way I'm going back to sleep.*

***

The new XO, Lt. Commander Masters, was in his forties, tall, and balding. His years at sea gave him an air of confidence. After dropping his gear in his cabin, he presented his orders to Theresa.

"Sit down, Commander," Theresa said, waving him to a chair. She looked at his personnel file and orders.

" Merchant marine for a while, then the regular navy. Bulk haulers and container ships, then a littoral combat ship, and shore duty before coming here. Pretty good. Do you have your master's license in the merchant marine?"

Masters shook his head. "I was a first officer before joining the Navy. If I'd stayed, I'd have my own ship by now."

"What did you do on the Littoral? Some of them didn't stay in service very long." Theresa commented, "Hull cracks and other problems, as I recall."

"Yes, Ma'am. They were supposed to be able to switch modules and handle a wide range of duties that would have required several ships to accomplish. A jack of too many trades. The modular design didn't work very well. I spent most of my time trying to make it work."

Theresa nodded, then handed him a folder. "These are my standing orders. My philosophy is pretty simple. Keep the bullshit to a minimum and leave the dress uniforms and spit-shined shoes in the locker until you need them. I prefer a light hand. Lead by example, crack the whip sparingly, and keep performance levels high. When I got here, the crew was used to heavy-handed bullying. It's going to take a long time to settle them down and rebuild their confidence. The Chiefs and lieutenants should try to handle minor disciplinary problems. If they don't, you hold them to the mark. If the infraction is serious and I need to crack a few heads, I'll do it.

"Have you ever seen any action? We've had a few incidents and close calls, but no more than anyone else."

"Mostly drills and training. Some live fire exercises."

Theresa nodded. "For the first few watches, I'll pair you up with an experienced officer of the day so you can get used to the things we deal with every day. If something happens, I expect you to take action and notify me. Use your own judgment. Lean on your OD or call me anytime with questions.

"Welcome aboard, Commander."

Theresa shook his hand. As Masters approached the door, he suddenly stopped and pulled an envelope from his pocket.

"I was told to hand deliver this to you, Ma'am."

Theresa looked at the envelope momentarily, keeping her face blank until Masters left.

It was from Rachel Nichol's solicitors.

***

"Lieutenant Ritter to the Captain's office, immediately!" the PA system blared.

Margot knocked on the cabin door before entering. Theresa was sitting behind her desk, looking at her.

"Lock the door."

Uh oh, this looks serious.

"Did you have anything to do with that?" Theresa pointed to the open envelope on her desk. Margot picked it up and looked at it.

Oh Shit!

"For heaven's sake, sit down and read it, Margot."

The letter said,

"At our client's request, we inquired into your concerns regarding Captain Nixon and Mrs. Nichol's husband, Joseph Nichols. The results of the inquiry were forwarded to Mrs. Nichols. She assured us she would be in touch with you shortly.

If we can be of further assistance in this matter, please don't hesitate to contact us."

Best Regards,

Laurence Gardner, esq.

"Uh," Margot started.

"Uh, is right. What did you do?" Theresa asked, a serious look on her face.

"Nothing...really," Margot said.

"You know there are sharks in these waters. You'd better come clean," Theresa said, leaning forward.

"I didn't like the way Nixon was treating you. It occurred to me that he was doing it for a reason. I figured Joseph Nichols had a hand in it."

"The rest, Margot," Theresa said sternly, waving a silver letter opener at her threateningly.

Finally, Margot gave in," Ok, when I mailed those letters to Matt for you, I added my own note asking him to ask Rachel to look into the possibility that her husband was pulling something. I asked her to go through Matt and me to keep you out of the loop in case it backfired. I don't know why they sent you a letter, too."

"I see," Theresa said," that's why Nixon was pulled off the Phelps and sent home, I bet."

"Could be," Margot admitted, looking at her feet and shrugging.

"So, you and Matt went behind my back and got Nixon fired," Theresa accused.

Margot shrugged.

Theresa opened the drawer on her desk and reached in. She took out the silver flask Margot had left under Theresa's mattress, tossed it to Margot, and said, "Thank you!"

Margot took a big swig of Irish whiskey and tossed the flask back to Theresa, saying," You're welcome, Therese."

***

Her new XO, Roger Masters, proved to be a friendly and experienced mariner. Once he came aboard, very few disciplinary problems came to Theresa's attention. Whenever possible, he took on as much of the commanding officer's paperwork load as he could without complaint.

Their teamwork did have its moments, though.

Theresa was used to taking quick navy showers, although, as captain, she could use as much water as she wanted. She had to shampoo her hair; it was getting pretty grody. As she stood there, soap in her eyes, she heard the warning announcement," General Quarters, General Quarters, inbound missile. Captain to the bridge!"

 A captain, especially one as beautiful and well-endowed as Theresa, couldn't jump from the shower and go to the CIC dressed in only a towel.

"Shit!" Theresa rinsed as much soap as she could from her hair, stepped into a pair of pants, and donned a T-shirt, pulling on her uniform blouse as she ran to the CIC. She hadn't arrived before the sound of a missile being launched roared.

She stood inside the CIC hatch unnoticed, water dripping from her hair as the weapons officer announced, "Missile intercept thirty seconds."

Somewhere over the horizon, an anti-missile missile struck the incoming threat. The boom from the explosion could be heard faintly in the CIC.

Theresa walked over to Masters.

" Report."

 A sailor, deeply involved in the ongoing incident, belatedly yelled, "CAPTAIN IN CIC."

"A launch from inland. My best guess is thirty miles. The apparent target was in the anchorage. Most likely one of those damn mobile missile launchers: Back in its hidey hole by now, I bet."

Masters was trying his best not to laugh as he observed his captain beside him. She was wet, her hair dripping, and her shirt misbuttoned. The kicker was the bare feet, though. He put his hand over his mouth, vainly trying to hide the smile.

Theresa noticed his mirth and replied, "I think I'll go finish my shower now."

"Yes, Ma'am," Masters said, though it was muffled through his hand.

***

"As soon as our relief arrives, we are heading home," Theresa explained to Matt. She was sitting cross-legged on her bunk, headphones on her head for privacy. Sophie was asleep, and Matt had Theresa all to himself, at least on the computer screen.

"We've been engaged almost nonstop since we got here. The crew has really taken shape. A lot of our anti-missile ordnance has been used and replaced at least once. It's been hairy at times, but it's been interesting."

Theresa realized Matt looked a little down. "Matt, I'm sorry. I've been pretty thoughtless. I know you'd rather be here if you could be. How's the new job coming along?"

"Fine, Therese. I'm getting into a lot more than I realized. Your upgrades will be generations ahead this time." Matt shifted his position uneasily, then said, " Remember last time I was going to tell you something, but you were interrupted?"

How could I forget? I was almost blown up again.

"There are a few things I need to discuss with you."

"I'm listening. Is everything alright?" Theresa said, a look of concern crossing her face.

"To be honest, no."

Matt pulled an envelope from a pile of papers on the table. "Margot put a note in one of your letters to me. Why didn't you tell me all that was going on?"

"I couldn't, Matt. I had no way to contact you, and I was confined to the ship. I told Margot not to do anything, but you know Margot."

"A couple of days ago, I got this letter from that asshole Joseph Nichols addressed to you." He held the embossed envelope up to the camera. "Do you mind if I open it?"

"Go ahead, please." Theresa hunched forward as if she could read the letter through the screen.

Matt read the letter to himself and shook his head grimly." This is what it says,"

Dear Commander Leslie,

Thank you for contacting my solicitors. I am once again in your debt. Their investigation found that Joseph had made a deal with Captain Nixon to make your life a living hell and ultimately ruin your career. In exchange, Nixon would receive his support when promotions to Rear Admiral were made. He guaranteed Nixon's first star if he got you sacked. I have passed the information on to Anthony (Admiral Kincaid) and a few of my closest friends. Captain Nixon has been recalled and will retire. He knows he will never get another command at sea and has no chance of further advancement.

As for my husband, he lied to me once again, saying he had no hand in what Nixon was doing. Nixon's own words, admitting his complicity, were played back to him by my solicitors.

He believes I am powerless since he has already been reelected for another term. He is wrong. I have released portions of the results of my solicitor's investigation into his sexual harassment of women to the press and every tabloid magazine I can think of. His career may survive, but the next four years will be hell.

He also forgets that I own all our properties and his classic automobiles and pay for his club memberships. I have had his access to all of those suspended. He must survive solely on his congressional pay for a period of one year, including legal expenses. If he does anything further against you or any other woman, he knows I will sell off his priceless cars to the lowest bidder, followed by anything else he holds dear.

You must think me a fool to continue loving Joseph. Perhaps I am. He wasn't always this way.

Cordially,

Rachel Nichols

Theresa sat back, considering what Matt had read. For a man like Nichols, this was a substantial slap-down.

*The scandal, lawsuits, and potential jail time are real,
knowing Rachel Nichols.*

"You know, I feel sorry for her being married to such a
sleaze. In her own way, she is trying to change him. Was
there something else we needed to talk about?"

Matt seemed to pause, debating something. Theresa
could read him most of the time.

He's hiding something.

"Actually, yes, though it's not as serious as that letter. Did
you tell Margot to get me a present?"

"Yes, it should have been sent when Sophie's doll was."

"Did you specify what she was going to buy me?" Matt
asked.

"Nooo, Theresa replied. *It must be something I'm going
to regret.*

Matt reached off-camera for a moment, returning with, of
all things, a hatbox. Theresa's curiosity was piqued as he
opened it and placed the large red conical hat on his
head.

"A FEZ? She bought you a fez!" Theresa laughed, falling
over on her bunk, holding her stomach. When Matt blew
the long tassel out of his face, Theresa was no more good.

"Laugh now, but I'm wearing it at our wedding," Matt
said.

"OH NO YOU'RE NOT!" Theresa squealed. Though not particularly funny in and of itself, after all the stress, destruction, and chaos of the last few months, the absurd sight of Matt wearing that traditional Arabic hat almost drove her to hysterics.

"I'm thinking of joining the Shriners. They wear these things, too."

CHAPTER 9

"Attention!" Theresa rose swiftly to her feet. Admiral Paul A. Larsen strode into the room, followed by a legion of aides. Theresa had been summoned to the Admiral's flagship along with several other captains, but had not been told why.

"At ease, sit down," Admiral Larsen said absently. The lights in the conference room dimmed.

"In November 2023, Houthi rebels boarded the car carrier Galaxy Leader,*** seizing it along with 25 hostages. Since then, it has sat virtually abandoned in Hodeida, Yemen. The crew has been released, so anyone aboard is likely an enemy and armed. Surveillance since the takeover shows that, at first, there was a large contingent of rebels on board. Maybe thirty. That number has steadily decreased the longer negotiations for the ship's release drag on. Intelligence suggests that there are probably ten armed guards on board at any given time now.

"The new administration in Washington has decided it is past time to take action.

"The mission is what they used to call a 'cutting out' mission in the old sailing days. A crew would row into a harbor by night, seize a ship, and sail it out or destroy it before the enemy could stop them. That is the essence of our task. The last time something similar to this was tried was when the SS Mayaguez was seized by the Khmer Rouge off Cambodia in 1975.

"The Galaxy Leader is owned by the British, so their SAS (Special Air Service) and SBS (Special Boat Service) will be responsible for seizing it. Our SEALs are tasked with backing them up if necessary, cutting the anchor cables, and checking the hull's exterior for any underwater explosives. The SEAL boats will provide local protection around the ship with their machine guns and cannons in case someone tries to interfere.

"The Galaxy Leader's power plant has been dormant for a little over a year. It is unlikely it could be started in time to be of any use in its escape; therefore, two fleet tugs will be used to tow it out of port to a safe anchorage.

"A carrier will provide aircap over the task group and strike designated targets in and around the harbor before the seizure. Anti-ship missile sites and harbor defenses are their primary targets.

"Ship drivers, you are responsible for attacking designated points in the harbor as well, including a known construction site for suicide boats. Should anything larger than a rowboat attempt to intercept the tugs as they enter or clear the harbor, you will destroy it. SEAL boats will carry GPS designators so you can tell friend from foe.

"Timetables and specific assignments are in the packets you'll be given. Any questions?"

Theresa joined the line to receive her packet. It wasn't thick, but it was thorough.

This is pretty bold! Theresa thought as she read through her ship's packet.

"Hello, Theresa," a voice said behind her.

Speaking of bold.

Lieutenant, now Lt. Commander James O'Brien, US Navy SEALs, strode up beside her.

"O'Brien! Congratulations on the promotion." She favored him with a cautious smile.

He hadn't changed much since their introduction on the Derecho.

"Want to celebrate it with me? I still owe you that drink," he said, casually slipping his arm around her waist. Theresa moved away.

"You never give up. Are you going to get your feet wet on this operation, O'Brien?"

They walked away from the chattering crowd.

"It's Jim and, officially, no. This is most likely my last deployment before a desk job in Coronado. Command responsibilities now."

"Too bad. I'm skipper of the Phelps. If all goes well, we'll rotate home after this."

"That drink is inevitable, you know," O'Brien said, moving closer to Theresa.

"I'm engaged now, Jim," she said, stepping away, smacking his chest with her packet of papers for emphasis. She walked over to a coffee urn and poured herself a cup.

O'Brien came back, much like a rubber band. "So? Let me guess: it's that lieutenant who wanted to fight me outside your cabin that day."

Theresa almost spat out her hot coffee. She looked at O'Brien in amazement.

O'Brien looked at her, seeing confirmation in her eyes. "How do I know? I've been a player all my life. The way you two looked at each other when you thought no one was watching told me there was something there. I heard how he reacted when you were wounded. It's not too hard to figure out. You're being naughty, Theresa."

"He's a civilian now," she replied, a little embarrassed at being detected so easily, "Naval reserve. We're getting married as soon as I get back."

O'Brien escorted Theresa to the helipad. The passageway was dimly lit, probably because of a blown electrical circuit in the wiring. When O'Brien saw that no one else was around, he stopped Theresa, placed his hand on the bulkhead above her shoulder, and leaned in to kiss her, his fingers playing with the buttons on her blouse.

"Careful, Commander, the last person who tried that got some broken fingers."

O'Brien stopped, shook his head, then slowly withdrew his hand. Theresa walked away unhurriedly.

As she walked down the passageway, O'Brien yelled, "Invite me to the wedding!"

 She stepped out on the helipad, holding her cap on her head against the wind from the helicopter blades. Theresa laughed and yelled back, "Not a chance! If I see you at an officer's club someday, though, the first round is on you!"

***

Theresa was in the CIC, counting down the minutes before her part of the operation began. The Phelps was off the coast near Hodeida, but over the horizon. It was pitch-black outside, and the lighting in the CIC was red to preserve everyone's night vision. They had been at battle stations for half an hour. The targets had been selected, and missiles targeted. Now, all she had to do was wait. When this cruise started, Theresa had been energetic, amped up for anything. These many months later, she was sobered by the thought of the death and destruction she was about to unleash. She walked out onto the bridge wing, looking toward Hodeida, anticipating the beginning of the battle. As she watched, the horizon began lighting up with flashes. In a moment, the distant sound of explosions reached her. Theresa returned to the bridge, took the sound phone off the wall, and said," CIC, this is the captain. Commence launch."

The sound of multiple missile launches rippling off, flame shooting from their tails, and the smoke drifting back over the bridge made it almost impossible for her to hear or see anything for the next few moments.

"OD, take us to our close-in station. I'll be in CIC."

The impact of the bombs and missiles striking so many targets in such a short time frame stunned the shore defenses. The SAS quickly overwhelmed the rebel security on board the Galaxy Leader as the two seagoing tugs approached. The car carrier was heading out of the harbor in less than fifteen minutes. SEAL crews silenced any resistance from shore installations. A boat coming toward the Galaxy Leader, apparently backup for the already dead security force on the ship, was strafed by SEAL boats making repeated high-speed passes and firing their heavy weapons. The luckless boat began drifting and burning as the tides pushed the dead crew back towards shore.

When all units finally cleared the harbor, the port was a smoking ruin; explosions from the suicide boat manufacturing facility lit up the sky. The mission had been an unqualified success.

Thirty minutes later, as the Phelps escorted the tug boats toward a safe harbor, the second phase of the battle began.

Radars across the fleet lit up with incoming threats of all types: missile launches, drones, and any remaining suicide boats attacked, centering on the Galaxy Leader.

"CAPTAIN! MULTIPLE MISSILE LAUNCHES, INBOUND MISSILES THIRTY MILES."

"CAPTAIN! PROBABLE SUICIDE BOATS INBOUND TWENTY MILES, CLOSING!"

Theresa yelled over the mayhem, "Everyone, quiet down! Report in your normal voice. You know the drill; we've been here before! RADAR- Look out for drones trying to slip into the mix. Target anything in our sector and prepare to engage."

"Here's where the fun starts," Theresa muttered sarcastically, unconsciously tightening her helmet.

 Beside her, XO Masters agreed, "Let us give thanks for what we are about to receive," giving voice to an old naval blasphemy from the days of sailing ships and broadsides.

Over the next hour, an intense battle ensued as rebels used every drone, missile, and suicide boat left to attack the Galaxy Leader and her escorts. Defense systems on the Phelps engaged targets and deployed countermeasures. Missile launches, cannon fire, machine guns, laser weapons, and even the last-ditch Phalanx systems engaged targets across the small fleet, creating a cacophony of deafening noise. The flagship coordinated fire from them all. Aircraft in holding patterns offshore engaged mobile missile sites as soon as their radars emitted signals.

For those on the Phelps's bridge, the night was filled with explosions, fireballs lighting up the small fleet from every angle. Radical steering commands followed rapidly as the ship struggled to evade incoming fire and bring weapons to bear.

The fleet did not go unscathed through the night. One aircraft was struck with an anti-aircraft missile as it pulled away from its target, the crew ejecting into the sea. Rescue helicopters were dispatched. Several ships in the fleet and the Galaxy Leader were struck despite the intense defensive fire. None were mortally damaged.

On the Phelps, a major portion of its surface-to-surface and surface-to-air anti-missile ordnance had been expended. The ship had survived the storm intact.

"XO, make sure the crew gets food. Rotate rest breaks in case there's a round three. You have the conn; I'll be in my cabin for a few minutes."

"Yes, Ma'am," Masters acknowledged. He turned to the officer of the day and said, "Tell the galley to fix up some sandwiches and drinks, anything else they can think of that we can pass out to crews on stations."

Before Theresa left the CIC, she paused. "XO, give me shipwide. I want to talk to the crew."

Masters handed her the mike. She leaned against the bulkhead for a moment, then pressed the button.

"Attention, this is the captain! I think I can safely say that we have just survived the most intense sea battle in recent naval history. We are staying at modified battle stations for now in case there is more coming our way. I'm proud of the way this crew handled the engagement. We accomplished our mission without casualties or major damage to anything but our eardrums. You people are the greatest. Thank you. That's it."

Theresa returned the mike to the XO and entered her sea cabin, closing the door and locking it. She didn't dare lie down, even for an instant, settling for splashing cold water on her face. She leaned over the sink with her eyes closed, listening to the water drip. Her whole body trembled as fear and adrenaline took their toll.

Thank you, God, for looking out for my crew and I and bringing us through this unharmed.

She took a few minutes to gather herself again, splashed more cold water on her face, and returned to CIC to give the XO a break.

***

News reports of the daring raid varied, depending on the source. In the Western media, the raid was a great triumph. In the Arab world, it was a heinous attack, killing mostly women and children and destroying only hospitals and other nonmilitary targets. Both sides knew the truth. The Houthis were embarrassed at losing the Galaxy Leader and the pounding their installations on shore took. The supposedly overwhelming counterattack had yielded very little except to reclaim some of the honor they'd lost.

Shortly after the raid on Hodeida harbor, the Phelps relief ship, the destroyer McCormick, arrived. It was time to go home.

***

It was their last port of call before leaving. Theresa wanted to go, but the report to the admiral on the Galaxy Leaders' mission would not wait.

"I'm sorry, Margot. I can't go. It seems I am fated never to set foot on shore this patrol." Theresa said regretfully.

"Ok, Therese. You could take a couple of hours, though. Just to say you have been on shore in an Arab country. There is so much to see!" Margot danced around a little, playing imaginary castanets with her fingers." It's worth being late on a report no one else will read. Everyone important already knows what happened. You can tell Sophie what it's like in the mysterious Middle East. You could buy a veil to match your wedding dress! Something exotic."

"Oh, Margot. You are such a ... I'll make you a deal. If I get this done before you are due back, I'll call your cell and meet you someplace, OK?"

"You think I'll be sober by that time? You are a pathetic optimist!"

Theresa laughed." If you ever get a ship of your own, you'll understand. Get going before I say 'the hell with it' and run down the gangplank with you!" Theresa laughed.

"Bye, oh boring one!" Margot laughed as she headed out the cabin door.

She's right, of course. I could take an hour or two and see the sights. This report could wait until we sail. Sometimes being responsible sucks.

CHAPTER 10

"Come in!" Theresa said, looking up from the mirror. It was early evening, the report had finally been sent, and Theresa was getting cleaned up so she could spend the last few hours on shore before they sailed. She was looking forward to exploring the port, at least for an hour or so. Masters said he'd be back early.

The officer of the day, Lt. Morgan, entered, saluting smartly and standing in front of her desk at attention.

"At ease, lieutenant. What do you want?"

"Ma'am, I wish to report that several officers returned to the Phelps intoxicated and out of uniform."

Is he serious?

"In what way, lieutenant?" Theresa replied, irritated that the OOD hadn't used a bit of discretion for his fellow officers and crewmen.

"Ma'am, they were carrying Lieutenants Ritter and Thomas up the gangplank. They were all disheveled in appearance."

Oh.

"Why are you telling me?" Theresa stated, "Who are you supposed to report to?"

"Ma'am, the Executive Officer, but he is on shore."

"And you couldn't wait for him to return this evening?"

"No, Ma'am," Morgan said. She looked at Morgan. His uniform was starched, with creases that could cut you if you were to touch them. Even his hat, duty sidearm belt, and holster were immaculate.

"Have you entered this in the deck log, lieutenant?"

"Yes, Ma'am."

SHIT! Theresa thought. *You will be real popular in the officers' mess this evening, Morgan. You've tied my hands, damn it. Now I have no choice.*

"Take their names, tell them they are restricted to the ship. They are to see me in the wardroom first thing in the morning. You too, Morgan."

"Yes, Ma'am," he replied.

About an hour later, the XO, Commander Masters, brought Theresa Morgan's report.

"These are half the junior officers on the ship, for God's sake! He put them all on report. How long has Lt. Morgan been on board, XO?" Theresa said angrily, tossing the file onto her desk.

"Nixon brought him aboard when he arrived. He isn't well-liked." Masters said.

"Small wonder. How many crewmen coming on board drunk from liberty have been disciplined? What are my options, XO?" Theresa asked. She leaned back in her chair, rubbing her eyes.

"Until now, it's only been the enlisted crew, maybe a handful. I've let their supervisors handle it unofficially. Usually, that means they get all the shit duty and maybe stand an extra watch, but nothing goes in their personnel jackets. This time, it's officers and on the record. The least they can expect is a written admonition. A written reprimand is the next highest. Either way, it's official. Of course, you can drop the whole thing if you want."

"That would look like favoritism to the crew, though," Theresa said, tapping a pencil on her desk in irritation.

"Probably," Masters agreed.

"Any enlisted men report drunk tonight?" Theresa asked.

"Not yet, Ma'am. Liberty is over in a couple of hours." Masters replied.

After Master's left, Theresa lay on her rack and contemplated.

All these officers, including my maid of honor, Margot, are on report. It will be part of their next evaluation and will follow them for the rest of their career. All because one hard ass was the officer of the deck today. What do I do?

***

0700. The next morning. Breakfast dishes had been cleared away in the Phelps' wardroom. Margot, Thomas, and a few other officers were standing at attention in front of Theresa and the XO, Commander Masters.

"This is an informal hearing into your conduct yesterday. This is not on the record unless you did anything that would justify formal disciplinary action. No minutes are to be taken. If, after this informal hearing, any of you feel you have been unjustly treated or wish to have a formal Captain's Mast that will be part of your FORMAL RECORD, let the XO know, and we will reconvene. Is that clear?"

"Yes, Ma'am," the assembled officers said as one.

"Lieutenant Morgan, read your report, please."

Morgan stepped forward and, in a loud voice, read his report, concluding with

"The above-listed officers were obviously intoxicated, Lieutenants Thomas and Ritter requiring other officers to support them as they walked up the gangplank. They were also improperly attired, reflecting poorly on this ship and the US Navy."

"Who is the senior officer amongst the accused?" Theresa said.

"Lieutenant Ritter, Captain," XO Masters said.

"I see. Lieutenant Ritter, step forward."

Margot stepped one pace forward, eyes boring straight ahead into the bulkhead behind Theresa.

Damn. It would be her. "Lieutenant Ritter, explain what happened."

"Ma'am, we went ashore yesterday morning. We walked through the port, rode camels just for fun, and wandered the bazaars. All the touristy stuff. After that, we hit a few bars inside the international port area so as not to offend the Muslim population. I guess we got carried away, Ma'am. I don't remember much after that."

"I see. Anything else, lieutenant?" Theresa asked.

"Not that I remember, Ma'am," Margot replied, her eyes still fixed on the steel bulkhead.

"Anyone else want to add anything?" Theresa asked, looking at each of the ensigns and lieutenants before her. No one moved.

"Very well. Step back, Lieutenant Ritter."

Theresa turned to Commander Masters. "Have any of these officers been before you for anything like this, XO?"

"No, Ma'am," Masters replied.

"Any disciplinary problems or failures to meet expected performance standards?"

Masters replied," No, Ma'am. These officers have had no problems before today."

"Very well," Theresa replied, standing up and straightening her uniform before addressing them.

"Ladies and gentlemen. To say I'm disappointed in your conduct as ambassadors of this ship and the Navy in general would be restating the obvious. Each of you is better than that.

"My decision is as follows. The XO will handle any charges of improper wearing of the uniform in a manner he sees fit. In future, I expect all officers of this ship to return dressed appropriately and in full control of their faculties. Is that understood?"

"Yes, Ma'am!" the officers replied loudly.

"Except for the two senior officers and Lt. Morgan, the rest of you are dismissed."

After the other officers filed out of the room, Theresa addressed Margot and Thomas.

"I am the most disappointed in you two. You are senior and responsible AT ALL TIMES for the conduct of those under you. Instead of fulfilling your obligations, you ran amok, forcing junior officers to help return you to the Phelps safely. How will that look the next time you are officer of the day and those very officers come up the gangplank being carried by others?"

Margot and Thomas stiffened as if they had been slapped.

"This has been a very hard patrol. The officers and crew depend on you to LEAD. We have not just destroyed targets in some fucking video game! We killed real people and destroyed real targets to fulfill our mission. All of that is on MY shoulders. YOU, as senior officers, share that responsibility! Junior, less experienced officers look up to you for guidance. To set standards they must meet. In combat, each of you has performed admirably. I have no question of your competency there. It is now, after the shooting has stopped, you fell flat on your face.

"From this moment on, I expect you to show the leadership I know you are capable of, both on and off duty.

"I will not permit another incident such as this to go unpunished. Is that understood?"

"Yes, Ma'am," both responded. Thomas's face was red, and tears were in Margot's eyes as the rebuke hit home. Margot looked like she wanted to say something, but she held back.

"I have decided that the XO should assign you each such additional duties as he sees fit for the next two weeks. If you don't think this is fair, you are entitled to a formal hearing in front of a formal Captain's Mast with someone you choose as your representative to plead your case. If you accept my judgment, you are still afforded the right to formal proceedings at your request. If that is your wish, let the XO know. Do you have any questions?"

"No, Ma'am," they both said quietly.

"Dismissed."

The two lieutenants left, feeling the sting of the dressing down they'd just received. Lt. Morgan turned to leave with them.

"Lieutenant Morgan," the XO said. "Who told you to leave?"

Morgan stopped, turning to face the XO. "Uh, no one, sir."

"Front and center, mister," Masters commanded.

Morgan's eyes widened as he tried to understand what was happening.

"I believe you heard my order, Lieutenant," Masters said sternly.

Morgan stepped in front of the table where Masters sat, standing stiff at attention.

"Did you understand the warnings that Captain Leslie gave to the officers concerning informal hearings and Captain's Mast proceedings?"

"Yyyes, sir," Morgan said, his voice quivering.

"XO, would you care to press charges against Lieutenant Morgan?" Theresa asked, leaning her hip against the wardroom table and crossing her arms in front of her.

"If you don't mind, Ma'am, I want to talk to Lieutenant Morgan first."

"Very well. Let me know what you decide." Theresa said as she left the room.

Theresa and Masters had discussed this very thing this morning before convening the informal inquiry. Morgan had not broken any formal rule, save one. His duty was to report to the XO, not the captain, except in an emergency.

Because he decided to bypass the chain of command and go directly to Captain Leslie on a minor matter that could have been resolved when the XO returned, he was technically violating the standing orders he had tried to enforce against others. Commander Masters wished to clarify his displeasure about Morgan's disturbing the captain on such a relatively minor matter.

Theresa could hear Master's voicing his displeasure to Morgan before she reached her cabin.

***

The next morning, the Phelps left port, heading for the USA.

Theresa had not seen or heard from Margot since the informal hearing. Theresa had been forced to slap down her dearest friend on the ship to display fairness and avoid rumors of favoritism when she dealt out punishment to other crew members. Theresa had decided not to have the sailors she knew were eavesdropping in the galley removed for the same reason. By now, the entire ship knew what had happened. Crew morale was a tricky thing sometimes.

No doubt Margot was still upset from the ass-chewing she had been given.

She is avoiding me, moping around somewhere else during meal times.

If she doesn't snap out of it soon, I'm going to have to track her down. I hate feeling responsible for her suffering. I had no choice.

***

"Lieutenant Ritter to the Captain's cabin," the PA system blared.

Enough is enough, Theresa decided. It had been three days since the informal hearing, and Theresa still hadn't seen Margot.

In a moment, there was a loud knock on the door.

"Come in," Theresa said. Margot came in, standing quietly in front of Theresa's desk.

"Sit down, Margot. Tell me what's chafing your ass," Theresa said, pointing at a chair.

"There's nothing wrong, Therese."

"Uh, excuse me if I don't believe you. When my best friend on this ship disappears from her normal haunts, not even showing up for breakfast, lunch, or dinner two days in a row, either you are constipated, have a venereal disease, or something else is bothering you. Sing, little bird."

Margot snorted, trying to stifle a smile. "It's just... I'm sorry I let you down, Therese."

"What did the XO give you as punishment?" Theresa inquired.

"Thomas and I got two extra officer of the day watches when we get to port. After any leave we might request. He also suggested we both attend AA meetings when we get back."

"Off the record, right?" Theresa checked.

"Yeah. Joe is going to find one for us to attend. We have to bring back a couple of slips as proof of attendance. After that, we can choose to go or drop it."

"Do you think that is unreasonable?" Theresa stood up, made a cup of coffee for each of them, and handed Margot hers.

Margot shook her head as she poured a little cream into her cup. "That speech of yours hit pretty hard. Imagine me being a role model."

"You will do fine. Now you see, you can't continue to get blind drunk like that. I have faith in you, Margot. In fact, I have a very important assignment for you myself." Theresa punched a few keys on her laptop, then motioned for Margot to step over.

"Between now and the day we dock, you and I are going to look at wedding dresses and bridesmaids' outfits. What do you think of these two?"

"Uh-uh. I ain't going to no hillbilly wedding. Pick again!" Margot laughed.

***

The cross-ocean trip seemed to go on forever. Every mile brought her that much closer to Matt and Sophie. Though Theresa tried to stay involved in their wedding plans, many of the details fell to Matt and his mom to work out. It was distressing, but she could do little about it from so far away. They chose a date, a church, and a reception venue. Theresa spent a lot of time online looking at wedding dresses and sending pictures to her mom for her opinion. Margot helped by taking her measurements so

Theresa could step into her wedding dress as soon as possible. She would have little time for fittings and alterations when they got back. They picked out bridesmaids' dresses and colors, too.

I don't even know if the chapel is big enough, if it smells of mold or something.

Brides make all the arrangements, find a caterer, and handle all the other minutiae involved in a wedding, except me. I feel left out of my own wedding.

***

"Only a couple more days, and I'll be home. I can't wait to see you." Theresa said.

Theresa was in her cabin talking to Matt on the computer before going to sleep. Now that they were out of the battle area, she could take a shower and wash her hair without fear of interruption. Her hair was wrapped in a towel, and her robe was tied around her. They'd already caught up on the wedding arrangements and each other's day-to-day happenings.

"I miss you too, Therese. It seems like the closer you get, the more anxious I am," Matt replied.

"Matt, is Sophie asleep? I wish I could have been there to tuck her in tonight."

"Yeah. I'm going to bed soon, too. Alone, unfortunately."

"I have a present for you. I was going to wait until I got back, but I can show it to you now if you like."

"Love to."

Theresa got up and made sure the cabin door was locked, then went back to the computer.

"Can you see me, alright?" She asked.

"Uh-huh," Matt said.

Theresa slowly took the towel from her hair, shaking it to fall on her shoulders wildly.

"Wish you were here to comb it out, Matt. It's such a mess," Theresa said, a sultry smile on her face. She slowly untied her robe, letting it fall open. Matt sat forward, intensely interested in what he was seeing. Theresa slowly pulled the robe open. She closed her eyes, put her hands behind her head, and swayed slowly, displaying her formidable charms to Matt.

"Would you like to see more, Matt?" Theresa said.

Matt clasped his hands, bringing them to his mouth, his eyes wide open." You bet. Please."

Theresa let her robe drop, slowly standing up and moving back so Matt could see her whole body. She slowly rotated, running her hands over herself as Matt watched from hundreds of miles away.

Matt began licking his lips, enjoying the show. "This is so unfair, Therese."

Theresa's smile just grew wider as she moved back towards her rack.

She lay on the bunk, propped up on one elbow, watching Matt's reaction on the screen. "Maybe if you are a good boy, I'll do this for you again tomorrow. Good night, Matt. Sleep well," Theresa said, smiling and blowing him a kiss before clicking off the lights

CHAPTER 11

The tugs deliberately moved the Phelps into her berth.
Theresa was on the bridge walkway, watching the
process. A lot had changed since the last time she left
port. The Phelps had left virtually overhauled and tested
for battle. After all this time, she was tired and needed
repairs, upgrades, and resupply. The crew had weathered
the storm and returned as a cohesive, experienced team.

They are as tired as I am, she reflected as she watched
the last moorings completed and a gangplank installed.
There would be reports, conferences, and all the
expected details of a ship captain's life, but there was
also leave and her wedding to look forward to.

*Technically, I have another year on the Phelps before
someone else takes over. The blue dress navy is always
waiting in the wings, though.*

A blur of motion on the dock broke Theresa's fugue. She
refocused, seeing something dressed in red, pigtails
flying, as it jumped up and down and waved frantically.

SOPHIE!

Matt, standing beside her in civilian clothes, was trying to contain Sophie's desire to run up the gangplank and find Miss Theresa.

This is the first time I've ever had someone waiting for me when I got home! Theresa smiled broadly, her emotions threatening to destroy the demeanor expected from a ship's captain. She waved back, blowing them a kiss secretly.

Roger Masters walked out onto the bridge wing and stood beside Theresa. He could see the little girl below waving frantically.

"Ma'am, the ship is secure, landlines connected. As soon as a few remaining tasks are completed, we can start allowing liberty."

Theresa knew all that - she had gone through the process many times on other ships. She looked at Masters curiously.

"I'll take the watch, Theresa; go hug that little girl before she falls off the pier."

For once, Theresa relaxed, grasping his arm in thanks before heading ashore.

It was all Theresa could do to return the salute and walk off the ship. In the background, she heard the announcement, "Captain leaving the ship." Before both of her feet touched the dock, Sophie leapt into her arms.

Matt was close behind her. The sweetness of their embrace and Sophie's constant chatter was etched into her heart forever.

Masters could hear the joyous screaming and see the long-awaited reunion unfold below. He smiled, remembering when his wife met him at the dock in San Diego for the first time, just like this. He watched as the three of them walked away together.

***

Sophie was finally worn out. Matt had let her stay up way past her bedtime, 'just this once', knowing that even if he'd put her to bed, she would be too wound up to sleep. By ten p.m., Matt was carrying her to her room. He and Theresa tucked Sophie into bed and kissed her goodnight, getting a hug each in return.

They'd decided to spend Theresa's first night back at her place because she had to be aboard the Phelps early. The XO had to catch his flight to the West Coast.

For now, Theresa was where she wanted to be: At home, free from the stress and strain of the last few months, and in the arms of the man she loved.

Matt took her hand, leading her to their bedroom. They shared a grin of anticipation, a desire to quench their bodies' needs after being apart for so long.

The bedroom was dark, lit only by scented candles placed strategically around it. The blanket and sheets were already turned down, and an ice bucket, champagne, and fluted glasses were on the dresser. Matt started to open the champagne bottle, but Theresa took it from his hands and shoved it back into the ice.

"You don't have time for that," she whispered in his ear as she ripped his shirt open, wrapped her arms around his neck, and passionately kissed him. In moments, they lay naked on the bed. All the emotions she had buried, the loneliness and longing, were finally freed. Had Sophie been awake or the neighbors been sitting outside, the sound of Matt and Theresa's lovemaking would have scared the hell out of them.

***

Matt and Theresa lay in bed, snuggling. The feeling of each other's bodies engendered a sense of closeness and security they'd missed for so long. All was right in the world again.

"I love you, Matt," Theresa said." I've missed you so much."

Matt kissed the top of her head, caressing her bare back gently, "I love you, too. It's too bad captain's quarters aren't coed; I could have visited you aboard ship." Then, more seriously," How was it out there?"

Theresa slapped Matt's stomach at his coed remark, but then took a moment to figure out what she wanted to say.

"I thought after that incident with the Mahan, I knew what combat was. I hadn't really been scared most of the time. This cruise on the Phelps was different. It was terrifying at times. I had to put on my best captain's face so the crew didn't see it on me. The fear, death, and destruction were on a much larger scale. Thank God I didn't lose anyone.

"Even when we were just escorting a tanker or monitoring the coast for threats, the strain never let up. Month after month, anticipating an attack coming at any time, day or night, was exhausting.

"But now," she said, squeezing Matt and giving him a loving smile," I'm home, everyone I love is safe, and all I have to concentrate on is the refit of the Phelps and forcing you to make an honest woman out of me!"

"You don't have to worry about that. I've spared almost no expense to give you a memorable wedding ceremony. The reception hall is going to be beautiful, and I've booked that cabin again."

"I'm sorry I couldn't help you get all that together," Theresa said mournfully." Half the fun of getting married was struggling with the details and finally winning. She'd had little to do with making it all happen and missed it.

"I know. Usually, the guy has no say in anything and just goes along with the program. You were in on all the major decisions, though. Between you and I and our moms, we will have a magnificent wedding day."

"You do remember we are taking Sophie and Julie with us this time, right? I loved our time there alone, but..."

"Already set. Judy and Ted are going to take advantage of the situation and go on a trip themselves. We'll be unpaid babysitters."

"I'm glad you don't mind. Having a family of my own is new to me. I can't seem to get enough of it for some reason."

"About the refit of the Phelps," Matt began.

"I'm sorry about having to focus on that for now. I won't get to see much of you for a while."

"Actually, that was something I wanted to tell you before. You'll be seeing a lot more of me than you think. I've been assigned to repair and upgrade the Phelps weapons systems while she is in port. You will be tripping over me all day until it's completed."

"How did you wangle that?" Theresa said, amazed. She sat up.

"I hope I never get used to seeing you naked like that, Therese."

Theresa ignored the compliment, giving Matt a mock, stern look, her hands on her hips.

"I didn't have to pressure anyone. I told them I knew the captain of the Phelps and that we worked well together. The rest is history. "

***

 The next few weeks were a whirlwind of activity. Theresa had to split her time between overseeing the refit, conferences and meetings, wedding dress alterations, and a host of other things. The closer the wedding date came, and the refit of the Phelps drew to a close, the more anxious Theresa became. Family responsibilities drained away any free time she might have had.

Theresa was deep into her paperwork when her cabin door opened. Margot walked in.

"Good afternoon, Captain Ma'am. Are you ready for your party tonight?"

It took Theresa a moment to refocus. "Tonight?"

"Your bachelorette party starts at 1900. We chipped in for a limo."

Damn.

"Margot, I don't know. I'm submerged in all this." A sweeping hand covered a desk heavily laden with files, papers, and empty coffee cups.

"Which will all be there when you get back. We're starting at my house, then hittin' the road until midnight.

If we see something juicy enough, we might get you laid, too."

Theresa laughed, shaking her head. "Don't count on getting me that drunk!"

Margot turned to leave, tossing a non-regulation salute for Theresa: "1900, my house. If you're late, we will leave without you."

With friends like Margot...

***

Theresa arrived at Margot's house a little early, only to find the party was already cranking up. She knocked on the front door and waited a moment. No one answered. She could hear the music blaring inside. When she opened the door, a solid wave of music, heavy on the bass, struck her like a physical force. Margot waved, killing the music and dragging her downstairs into the living room. There were a few women she knew from her blue dress Navy days: Judy, her sister, Matt's Mom, Beverly, and Admiral Kincaid's secretary, whose name eluded her at the moment. In one corner, a food table and liquor bar were set up. On the other corner, there was a table with gifts. The air filled with music and laughter; the remains of plates and cups of every sort soon covered most of the end tables. Jello shooters served in condoms made the rounds. Everyone wanted to see Theresa's engagement ring. It was the first time she felt safe wearing it since Matt had given it to her. She was proud to show it off. When the time came to open the gifts, Margot sat Theresa on the couch and started passing boxes to her. Cell phone cameras caught every angle as Theresa opened the first. She pulled out a thin, lacy nightgown and a small patch of white cloth.

"The nightgown is beautiful, but what's that? "Theresa asked, pointing to the cloth. Margot unfolded the fabric and held it up.

 "It's either a lace handkerchief or the panties for that nightie!" After she looked at it closer, Margot said," I hope it's a handkerchief because it wouldn't cover much more than your nose."

"Open this one next," Judy cried, handing Theresa a long rectangular box.

I bet I know what that is!

When Theresa opened the box and slid its contents out, she thought she had guessed right. It had male appendages on either side. She gave Judy a look usually reserved for wayward children.

"It's a rolling pin! You have a dirty mind, Theresa!" Judy said, laughing. Theresa tried it, holding on to both ends. The center did indeed roll.

"You are unbelievable, sis!" Theresa said, laughing.

"Time to load up! The limo is here!" Margot yelled.

***

Theresa arrived at the Phelps on time. She saluted the officer of the day and the flag, then headed straight for her cabin.

Jello shooters. Flaming shots of God knows what, and I only slept for three hours when I got home. This day is going to be a bitch.

Once they'd left Margot's house, they rode in the stretch limo, drinking champagne, laughing, and gossiping. Their first stop was a place called the "Tea Room." Despite the genteel name, it was a male strip club. Young, virile men who wasted little time removing their outfits and dangling as much of their wares as allowed by law danced in front of them. Someone let slip that Theresa was about to be married. From then on, she was front and center of every act that came on stage. The male review wore what could generously be called a jock strap. They were soon festooned with dollar bills. Someone paid one particularly handsome fellow to give Theresa his version of a lap dance.

Where they went after leaving the "Tea Room" was a blur to Theresa.

At least Margot got me home on time. There's no way I could drive home after that.

Fortunately, Matt had begun updating the Phelps weapons array and could give her a ride to the ship.

Around 0900, Margot came in to check on Theresa. She was disgustingly happy for someone who had matched Theresa drink for drink all night.

"I hate you," Theresa said, her head resting on her desk and arms.

"Uh-huh. I didn't know you were such a lightweight. I just came by to check on you."

"I'll live, maybe."

By now, it was no secret on the ship that Theresa and Matt were engaged. Though decorum was observed at all times, they could freely discuss whatever they wished over lunch. The wedding plans had solidified, Sophie was doing well in school, and Admiral Kincaid had assured her that she would still command the Phelps for another patrol when the destroyer was ready.

***

"Captain! Incoming missile, ten miles!" Theresa was sitting in her captain's chair on the bridge of the Phelps. She was terrified. She struggled, but she couldn't move or say anything.

"Captain! Five miles! Please! Do something!" the young lieutenant pleaded. She could see the missile now, the Houthi flag waving proudly from on top as it got nearer and nearer. Everyone on the bridge was staring at her, praying for their deliverance.

"I'm sorry," Theresa said quietly as it impacted the bridge.

***

"Therese! Therese, wake up! It's OK, everything is ok."

Theresa kept struggling and screaming until she finally emerged from the dream. Matt was holding her, rocking her gently, a look of concern in his eyes.

"Matt, I..." Theresa started to say, her whole body trembling.

Matt did his best to console her." I know, baby. I know. It's okay now. Can you tell me about it?"

Nightmares, mostly of missiles heading toward her or suicide boats, terrified her night after night. They all had two things in common- she couldn't move, and they always killed her. Matt had insisted she see a doctor. The doctor gave Theresa medication and sleeping pills and recommended talking to a counselor.

"Matt, you're bleeding!" Theresa said, touching his busted lip.

"You were pretty energetic for a while. My face got in the way. I'm ok, sweetie."

Tears began running down her face as she lay her head back down on his chest. "I'm sorry, Matt. I didn't mean to..."

"I know, Therese. You can't help it. If someone asks, I'll tell them I got mugged by a female orangutan with a good right cross."

Theresa chuckled and sniffled, "That's so lame. You don't have to lie. Tell them we were having rough sex. Everyone will believe that."

Theresa hugged Matt tightly, "Why does this have to happen now? We're getting married in a couple of days. I have everything I want. I couldn't be happier."

"Remember what the counselor told us. You buried your fear so you could cope with the things you had to. Now that you don't have to do that anymore, it's coming out," Matt reminded her, softly stroking her head. "You'll be fine once you learn how to deal with it."

"I'm so afraid I'll scare Sophie one of these times."

"I've already told her that you have nightmares sometimes and not to get alarmed. If you want to tell her what you are going through in more depth, I think she will understand. We can have a family talk at dinner one night."

"I'd rather not unless it becomes an issue. I don't want her to be afraid every time I go away."

Theresa kissed Matt's chest and held him tight until they drifted off to sleep again.

As long as I have you, I can deal with anything.

CHAPTER 12

Today is the day. We're getting married. It's funny. Matt and I have been living together since I returned from Yemen. So why am I so nervous and excited at the same time?

It was a clear, warm day, perfect for a June wedding. Matt, Sophie, and Theresa sat at the breakfast table. Matt had made Sophie's favorite- pancakes with fruit on top, and she was busy eating. Matt and Theresa couldn't help smiling at each other as they sipped their coffee.

Theresa's parents, Sam and Martha, had flown in from their retirement villa in Florida. They were both in their sixties but still full of life. Gray hair never stopped them from doing what they wanted to do. They were staying at a local hotel to give Matt and Theresa privacy. It was the first time they'd met Matt and his parents. Martha and Sam fell in love with Sophie instantly. The rehearsal and the rehearsal dinner had gone off magnificently. Even Matt's dad, Sid, seemed to be upbeat.

"Matt, I was beginning to worry Theresa would never get married," Martha, Theresa's mother, said. "Since she was a little girl, she always had her eyes set towards the horizon. I wasn't too surprised when she picked the navy over all the other offers she had."

"I don't doubt it. It took me accidentally dunking my phone at the beach one day to get her attention. She is so independent. I think Sophie sealed the deal. Once Theresa sampled what she could have, nothing could dissuade her. She persevered until, after all she has gone through to get to this moment, she finally has both a career and a family. The best of both worlds."

The church on base they'd decided to use was designed for all faiths. It had been adorned over time with flowering bushes, moss, and similar embellishments. It hadn't been updated or sandblasted in years, giving it an old, comfortable appearance. Matt had been authorized to wear his Naval Reserve dress uniform whites. Theresa could have worn her uniform also, but there was no way she would miss out on wearing the beautiful wedding gown she had picked out.

***

"It's that time, Therese," Margot said, adjusting Theresa's veil. "Go get married."

"I'm feeling..." Theresa said. Everything was ready; the organ prelude was starting. *And I want to throw up.*

"Scared." Margot finished for her." I was, too. You have waited all this time for this moment, and now you are overwhelmed. When I got to this point, I felt like running. I'm glad I didn't. You look lovely. Go grab your dad's arm and go meet your new husband."

Theresa stood up, looking into the full-length mirror one last time. Her gown was white, featuring a sweetheart neckline, a brocaded waist, and a short train at the back. A string of pearls was tight around her neck. She held a bouquet of white and pink flowers. The hairdresser had set her braids high on her head, and a silver tiara and short veil held them all in place. Theresa smiled to herself, turned, and went to meet her father.

"You look lovely, my dear," Sam, her father, said,

"A vision in white. Are you ready?"

"Oh yes, Dad," Theresa said, "Scared, but ready." The hands on the clock ticked down until at last, it was time.

***

Matt stood at the altar in his formal dress whites. He'd left the sword in the car.

I can see myself tripping on that thing on the way out.

The music changed suddenly. The beautiful notes of the wedding march began to play. Matt had seen Theresa dressed (and undressed) in many ways, from official ship captain to bikini-clad beauty. Today, she was a picture of elegance. Breathtakingly beautiful. She was on her father's arm, slowly making her way down the aisle to him. A few feet in front of them, Sophie, the flower girl, was supposed to be spreading flower petals on the floor as they walked to the altar. She was pitching them by the handful in all directions instead. Theresa tried not to crack up, but Matt just had to laugh. At last, Mr. Leslie kissed Theresa, giving her hand to Matt, and sat down.

"Dearly beloved, we are here in this company and in the sight of God to join Matt and Theresa in the holy bonds of matrimony." The chaplain droned on and on, seemingly forever. Finally, the words they most wanted to hear.

"Matthew, do you take Theresa for your lawfully wedded wife?"

Matt looked deeply into Theresa's eyes, "I do, with all my heart."

He placed the ring on her finger gently, lovingly.

"And do you, Theresa, take Matthew as your lawfully wedded husband?"

"I do, with all my heart."

Theresa placed the wedding band on Matt's hand, squeezing his hand in hers.

"Matthew and Theresa, I now pronounce you man and wife."

 Matt and Theresa leaned in for their first kiss as husband and wife, and a feeling of unbounded joy filled them.

"Yippee!" Sophie yelled, jumping up and waving her hands in glee as Beverly tried to drag her back to her seat.

***

 Matt and Theresa braced themselves as they stepped out onto the church's front steps. Ranks of their friends lined the sidewalk on either side. Behind them, the head usher yelled the preparatory command, "DEERAAAW!" The officers, clad in immaculate dress white uniforms, on either side of the walkway, reached as one for the swords at their waists. "SWORDS!" The metallic sound of swords being drawn from scabbards filled the air, and the sword arch was quickly formed.

As soon as Matt and Theresa started down the steps, volleys of birdseed pelted them. They laughed, trying to keep the seed out of their face and hair until they reached the limousine parked at the curb.

"I can't believe it! We're finally married!" Theresa squealed, wrapping her arms around Matt as the limo pulled from the curb. Matt kissed her passionately, inhaling the intoxicating fragrance of the Royal Bay Rhum in her hair.

The reception was held at the Veterans of Foreign Wars Hall, fittingly. When the limousine pulled up, the veteran's group had its honor guard waiting to greet them. Matt's father, Sid, in full dress uniform, escorted them into the hall.

"You look beautiful, Theresa," he said, kissing her on the cheek.

"Thank you, Sid. I feel on top of the world today," Theresa said as they were waiting to be announced at the main doors to the hall. "My jaws hurt from all the smiling!"

"After all you've been through the last two years, you've earned it. Matt, you better treat her right, got me!" Sid said, straightening Matt's tie.

"Yes, sir, Chief, I will," Matt replied.

The master of ceremonies looked through the window at Sid. Sid nodded and opened the door.

"Ladies and gentlemen, may I introduce to you for the first time, Mr. and Mrs. Matthew Chapman! Bosun! Pipe them aboard!"

As Matt and Theresa walked into the hall, a retired Bosun's mate, whose belly almost exceeded the capacity of his struggling uniform shirt buttons, sounded his pipe until they sat down at the head table. Theresa turned to Margot with a look that said, *REALLY?*

Margot shrugged, smiled, and blew Theresa a kiss.

Matt leaned towards Theresa and whispered," You know Margot!"

"Yes, I do! I should have figured she'd do something like that!" Theresa laughed.

On the way home on the Phelps, Theresa and Margot had argued about Theresa's gown and the bridesmaids' dresses. If Margot had had her way, Theresa's gown would have displayed her breasts prominently, the neckline dipping indecently low. "I'm not wearing body tape on my boobs, Margot."

They'd compromised on the bridesmaids' gowns, though they both agreed "No blue dresses!"

Theresa laughed as the sound of spoons

banging on glass filled the room.

They didn't stop until Matt gave her a long, gentle kiss, as the crowd roared.

Matt held Theresa close as they danced their first dance as a couple. They'd picked a slow dance so that they could enjoy the moment. Theresa looked around the room, a sea of white uniforms and ball gowns in a variety of colors. There wasn't one blue ball gown anywhere. Margot had passed the word.

"This is so heavenly, Matt. I've waited so long for this day." Theresa said, laying her head on his shoulder and feeling him hold her tight.

"I know. It took a lot to get here, but we did it. I love you, Theresa."

"I love you too, Matt."

The parents' dance came next. Theresa's dad gliding her around the floor.

"I'm so happy for you, Theresa. I haven't known Matt long, but you two seem to fit together so well."

"I wish you and Mom could have met him sooner, but with our deployments not meshing, we couldn't get a week we could both take off and fly down."

"I imagine there will be a lot of that. One or the other, maybe both of you, deployed at the same time. It won't be easy."

"We'll make it work, Dad. You might have to fly here once in a while, but we will see you as often as we can."

They stopped to watch Matt dance with Sophie. They were twirling slowly around the dance floor together, Sophie laughing as he swung her in the air.

"You've got a good start to your family, Theresa," her dad said.

"I know," Theresa replied. She felt a tap on her shoulder. She turned around to see Sid standing there, with a smile on his face. *Sid smiling! It must be a special day!*

"Congratulations, Theresa. Welcome to the family," Sid said as they began their dance.

"Thanks, Sid. That means a lot," she replied.

"All those years in submarines, we never fired a war shot. Hiding in the depths, either tracking Russian submarines or avoiding them. You come along and blow the hell out of terrorists all over the world. I am impressed," he said grudgingly.

"Still think women don't belong in the Navy?" Theresa teased as the song came to an end.

"Hell yes!" Sid replied." But you'll do."

***

The wedding cake had several layers: basic white buttercream frosting with blue and gold trim on each layer, multicolored flowers circling around the bottom, and a naval officer holding hands with his bride on top.

Matt and Theresa held Matt's sword so the photographer could snap a formal picture. From the back of the crowd, someone yelled,

"Are you going to make him salute you when you get home tonight, Theresa?"

"Hell no, she's going to make him scream pretty loud, though!" Margot yelled back, just as the photographer snapped the picture. The picture had to be retaken, but the one with Matt laughing and Theresa covering her face became their favorite wedding picture.

***

 Matt and Theresa sat on the porch in the moonlight, watching Sophie and Theresa's niece Julie roasting marshmallows on the crackling fire. They were tired but happy. The moon and the endless stars gave them a sense of peace. The mugs of steaming hot tea they held were a perfect way to end the day.

"What are you thinking, Theresa?" Matt asked, blowing on his tea.

Theresa paused for a moment, sipping her drink.

"I was thinking how lucky I've been these last couple of years. I met and married the most loving, caring man in the world. I have a daughter I absolutely adore. I've got my own ship, at least for another year. I'm sure I'll be posted on shore after that, at least for a while, but not here, not in the blue dress navy. Life is almost perfect."

"Almost?" Matt inquired.

Theresa nodded, cradling Matt's hand in hers, looking deeply into his eyes, smiling naughtily.

"Do you think Sophie would mind having a little sister?"

THE END

*The Caine Mutiny, 1954 Herman Wouk

  ** December 6, 1917. World War 1. The French ship SS Mont-Blanc, laden with high explosives and enroute to France, collided with the Norwegian ship SS Imo in Halifax harbor. The resulting fire and explosion devastated everything within a half-mile perimeter of the ships. Buildings collapsed, and 1,782 people were killed. Another 9000 were wounded in the blast. The resulting Tsunami drove ships aground and created additional widespread devastation.

Source: Wikipedia.

***The MV Galaxy Leader, a roll-on roll-off car carrier, was seized by Houthi rebels in November 2023. As of this writing, it is still anchored in Hodeida, Yemen.

Website "Not What you think." 9/19/25

US Navy vs Houthi video

"How Houthi's nearly maxed out US Navy air defense."

ACKNOWLEDGEMENTS

A big thank you to my wife Lynn- for her critiques and patience, and-

Dana Symborski Conigliaro- for her sharp eyes and straight talk.

These two ladies helped keep my manuscript on track, making the final product much better than it would have been otherwise.

Md Mushfequzzaman/ Dreamstime.com for the anchor illustrations.

Evgeniya G., for such a wonderful cover.

Bykota Writing Club - For suggestions and help with formatting.

AUTHORS BIOGRAPHY

Walter King is retired. He lives in the Baltimore, Maryland, area with his wife, Lynn, mother-in-law, Betty, and their dogs, Mila and Maggie Mae.

His first book, "Clay's Journey," is available on Amazon.

OTHER BOOKS BY WALTER KING

"Clay's Journey"

Help is almost here, Mark. Keep pulling!"

The force of the explosion slammed Clay back; his flight suit was a mass of flames.

Clay Washburn was a 20-year Army Special Forces veteran looking forward to retirement. A tragic accident leaves him horribly scarred and struggling with visions of terror. Alcohol addiction is destroying his career. He signs on for a modern-day cattle drive, hoping that fulfilling a childhood dream will help him rebuild his shattered life.

Barbara Mitchell is a 29-year-old riding instructor. Her whole life revolves around horses. She and her sister Sherry are eager to test their skills on a modern cattle drive.

Clay and Barbara grow closer together as the drive progresses. Barbara has sworn to be celibate until marriage, but her resolve is severely tested as their love grows.

 Betrayal and murder force Clay and sisters Barbara and Sherry, into a struggle for survival. Clay must use his experience and skill to keep them alive while merciless killers pursue them in the backwoods of Oklahoma.

Clay and Barbara are unaware that other, equally dangerous forces are waiting to destroy their plans for a future together.

"Clay's Journey" is a contemporary adventure-romance story.

"Forever Amelia"

On July 2, 1937, Amelia Earhart and her navigator, Fred Noonan, left Lae, New Guinea, on the last leg of their attempt to circumnavigate the world. They disappeared somewhere over the vast Pacific Ocean.

Eighty two years later, the yacht, "Sarah Bee," strikes a reef and sinks during a typhoon, stranding Denise West and deckhand Justin Meadows on a remote island in the Pacific Ocean. The lavish life Denise once knew is gone, shattered by betrayal and her knowledge of the real reason the Sarah Bee sank.

Denise must learn to work with Justin if they are to survive. Together, they learn the solution to an eight decades old mystery: What really happened to legendary American aviator Amelia Earhart?

The answer affects their lives in ways they could never have imagined.

If you're looking for adventure and romance, "Forever Amelia" is the perfect book for you.

The US Coast Guard Cutter Taney (WHEC-37) is a museum ship docked at Pier 5 in Baltimore's Inner Harbor. It is one of the last ships afloat to fight during the attack on Pearl Harbor, Hawaii, on December 7, 1941.

Other historic ships at the Inner Harbor include the WW2 submarine Torsk, the lightship Chesapeake, and the sloop of war Constellation.

The Seven Foot Knoll Lighthouse is also displayed at the Inner Harbor.

All are open for public tours daily.